W9-DFE-598

By Sherril Jaffe

Scars Make Your Body More Interesting (1975)
This Flower Only Blooms Every Hundred Years (1979)
The Unexamined Wife (1983)
The Faces Reappear (1988)

SHERRIL JAFFE

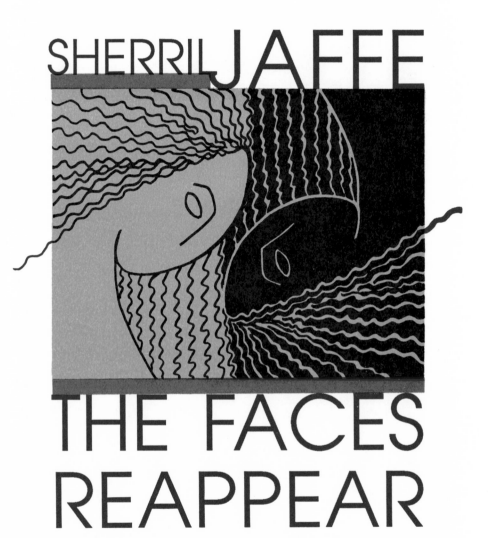

THE FACES REAPPEAR

BLACK SPARROW PRESS   SANTA ROSA   1988

Library of Congress Cataloging-in-Publication Data

Jaffe, Sherril, 1945-
  The faces reappear / Sherril Jaffe.
      p.   cm.
    ISBN 0-87685-711-X : ISBN 0-87685-710-1 (pbk.) :
  ISBN 0-87685-712-8 (signed cloth) :
    I. Title.
  PS3560.A314F3   1988
  813'.54—dc19   87-29526
                                          CIP

for Hannah and Malka

THE FACES REAPPEAR

Up into the Cherry Tree
Who should climb but little me?
I held the trunk with both my hands
And looked abroad on foreign lands.

—Robert Louis Stevenson

I. View from a Foreign Land

The Memory

THE SKY was bright. The sidewalk was divided into squares. On one side there was a square of grass which separated the sidewalk from the curb. On the other was a square green hedge. Ann walked along looking at the hedge, the sidewalk, the grass and the curb. She was looking for money. Once she had found a five dollar bill in a hedge. Or had she dreamed it? It was an ordinary day, a day in which nothing in particular was happening. She thought about her life and tried to remember what it had been. She was only seven years old, but how little she could remember. She could remember almost nothing of her first years on earth. She had not thought to commit them to memory; now they were gone. She closed her eyes and promised herself she would always remember this moment.

At the Edge of Her Vision

ANN LAY IN BED in the dark though the light was burning in the hall. She was hoping that the dots would come again— red and orange and blue and green pin-pricks of color floating through the dark. Now she sees them out of the corner of her eye—bright dots of color swimming swiftly through the blackness. She wants to follow them but if she looks at them directly they will go away. Now they are gone. Now they come again, beautiful bursts of color flying in the dark at the very edge of her vision.

The Black Automobile

IT WAS NIGHT. Speech had given way to the droning of the automobile. A black automobile. Ann sat in the back seat. She could not see her mother and father who sat in the front. Her sister Barbara was lost in shadows opposite her. The seat was deep. The window was high above. Through the window lights flashed from time to time. They sliced into the dream of the world and then they were gone.

Why Do They Break
If They're Unbreakable?

BARBARA STOOD on the back steps throwing round black records onto the concrete in the yard. "They're unbreakable! Unbreakable!" she screamed. Then they broke. "Why do they break when they're unbreakable?" she yelled. Everyone was ganging up on her. She snatched Ann's teddybear, Da-doo, and started to throw it into the yard. Ann clutched her heart, afraid that it would break.

The World Suffused with Light

THE COMFORTER was a peachy satin with rosy satin flowers. It was snapped inside a cotton coverlet covered with small pink flowers. Ann crawled inside and snapped the coverlet shut. She rolled around and around until the feathers began to fly. Then she lay back and the feathers floated down all around her. Ann could not see through the cotton coverlet, but the light from the window shone in, and the feathers floated in the rosy golden light. This world suffused with light—Ann was not supposed to play here.

The Rock Moves

ANN WAS WALKING along in the forest minding her own business. But she was tired. She saw a nice inviting rock, just right for sitting on. "I think I'll sit down on this rock!" she said, and she did. Then the rock began to move. It moved and it moved until it pushed Ann off. "What's this?" she asked. "How can a rock move?" She climbed back on, but the rock moved and moved until she was off again. Then Barbara climbed out from under the blankets. Now it was Ann's turn to be the rock.

The Figurine in the Dust

ANN DID NOT WANT to take a nap. She was not able to sleep, but terrified to let the teacher know. She pretended to sleep. She was afraid. She missed her mother and father. Everyone here was strange. The rug they had to sit on scratched her. She was walking along the fence poking in the dirt and feeling miserable when she saw it — a perfect figurine in the dust.

In a Saucer of Water

ANN WAS ON TOP of the refrigerator. From here she could survey the entire kitchen—the counter where she lay flat on a towel while Mommy washed her hair in the sink, the window sill over the sink where her and Barbara's carrot ends sat in a saucer of water sending out transparent roots, the cupboard below with its door slightly ajar where the blackened pans with their sharp corners that she and Barbara took to bed with them when they were sick could just be glimpsed and next to them the lime green bowls of the Mixmaster and the ghost of Mommy standing on the red linoleum peeling potatoes and handing Ann down a small piece.

The Banana Lady

ANN HAD SEEN the picture of the Banana Lady in the Sunday comics. The Banana Lady was a doll in the shape of a banana who was also a beautiful lady. Ann loved the Banana Lady and wanted her so badly that she finally had her. She had fruit on her head. She was smiling and laughing. It was in the den on the green rug in her Aunt Lil and Uncle Jack's house that Ann realized that she didn't have the Banana Lady. Where had she gone? Had she lost her already? She was crying, bereft and terrified that she had never really had her at all.

How the Rabbit Felt

ANN'S RABBIT, Fluffy, had disappeared. It had hopped through a hole in the hedge which separated their yard from the yard of the people who lived around the corner on another street. Ann did not know who these people were, but she disliked them because they always played opera on Sunday afternoons and it leaked through the hedge. The hedge which separated their yards was also a bee bush. It had flowers that Ann liked to suck for the honey, but she was always afraid of the bees. Now she had to go around the corner to another street and knock on the door of a strange house to ask if her rabbit was in their back yard. The strangers led her to the back garden. They were actually very nice. There was her rabbit. Ann felt a rush of relief. She picked it up and put it on a lawn chair. Then it peed, a thick lemon yellow pee over everything.

Ann Loses Mommy

ANN AND MOMMY were wearing identical mother and daughter dresses. Ann walked behind Mommy into the department store. Perfume floated in the air. Bells rang. People went up and down the escalators. The elevator doors opened and shut. Light shot from the glass cases as they passed. Women were pawing through mounds of gloves, sweaters, purses. The clothes hanging on the racks shouted at the people walking by. Ann bumped into someone and said "excuse me," but it was only a statue. She saw a man in a dark suit standing in the middle of the floor. He was looking at her. She ran to catch up with Mommy and reached for her hand. "Mommy!" she called. Then Mommy turned, but a stranger's face looked down at her.

The Huge Man's Head

ANN WANTED TO play ball with the big boys in the yard with
the dusk just falling, one of them throwing the ball overhand
from the garage to where Ann stood on the back step, and
it hit her between the eyes. Now they no longer played in
the yard but in the big empty lot with its emerald grass two
blocks away at the edge of the boulevard. Ann never saw
them play there, though she knew they did. When she went
up to the boulevard she looked for them, but they were never
there, and she stood by the understructure of the huge
billboard which looked out at the busy boulevard and she
looked up at the huge man's head.

Where They Were Heading

ANN WAS RIDING a golden palomino. Her cowboy hat was pushed back from her head. Next to her rode a handsome cowboy. Their horses were in perfect step. They galloped through the purple sage into the west. The sun was just sinking behind the western hills. Ann woke up. As soon as she knew she was awake sorrow filled her. Why did her dream have to end? She closed her eyes and lay back on the pillow. The red curtains began to open. Ann was riding a golden palomino. Her cowboy hat was pushed back from her head. Next to her rode a handsome cowboy. Their horses were in perfect step. They galloped through the purple sage into the west. The sun was just sinking behind the western hills where they were heading.

Ann Has No Choice

ANN SAT ALONE at the table. It was a little table, just for her and her sister. They were not allowed to sit at the big table because Barbara kicked her feet. She kicked Mother.

There was a plate in front of Ann at the table. On this plate sat several green peas, cold and disconsolate. Ann was not allowed to leave the table until she had finished her peas. But she was not going to touch them.

It wasn't that she wanted children to starve in China. She didn't care. It wasn't that she disliked peas. She liked them as well as anything. It wasn't that she was willful and stubborn. She couldn't expect her mother to understand. She had no choice. Barbara had breathed on them.

The Wish

ANN WISHED she were small. Small enough to crawl into a mousehole. There she would have a little bed made out of a matchbox. Or a sardine can. She would be able to crawl into her mousehole and nobody would be able to follow her. She would overhear conversations in the room but it would be as if she wasn't there. True, she wasn't very large. Just too large to fit into a mousehole. Once she had been small enough. But she had not known how lucky she was. How she regretted the past! Only by wishing, now, could she fit there.

Barbara Holds Up the Mirror

ANN SAT ON A CHAIR in the center of the yard. There was a sheet tied under her chin. Only her head stuck out. Her sister Barbara held a pair of scissors and laughed. She had made Ann's bangs a little ragged. She would have to even them up. Barbara stood back holding the scissors. She laughed. One side was shorter than the other. She would have to even them up. She laughed, brandishing the scissors. Ann's bangs were still uneven. What there was of them. The sun glinted off the scissors. Daddy was just coming home from a trip. He was climbing the back steps in his blue suit and black shoes. Ann sat powerless under the white sheet. Barbara held up the mirror to reveal Ann's humiliation. Then Daddy gave Ann the teddy bear.

Daddy Disappears

THEY WERE ALL enjoying breakfast when Daddy got up to leave. He picked up his briefcase and bent over Mother to kiss her. Then he kissed Barbara. Then he kissed Ann. The kiss was wet and horrible. "Ugh!" Barbara said. "Daddy kissed me. Do you like those wet kisses?" she asked Mother. "No," Mother said. Daddy was disappearing from the narrow kitchen.

Bright Red and Orange

ANN STOOD on the low concrete ridge that rose on the edge of the driveway. She was holding onto the wire of the fence and looking into the neighbors' yard. In the middle of that yard stood a broad palm tree. Its bark was like shingles. Many were loose. Its fronds hung low around the house it created. Bushes grew all around, green and impenetrable. Ann walked along the ridge, carefully placing one foot in front of the other, hoping that she wasn't being observed from her own house. Her own house had been taken over by witches. Inside, there were no longer any rooms, only narrow corridors painted bright red and orange.

Daddy's Quiet Breathing

ANN WAS CRYING in her bed. She had had a nightmare. But it was real. The house had been taken over by witches. Finally Daddy came in to comfort her. But it was too late. She couldn't stop crying. She was sobbing convulsively. She no longer wanted to stop crying. Finally Daddy got into bed with her. Now Ann was safe. Her sobs began to subside. She grew quieter and quieter until all she could hear was Daddy's quiet breathing.

The Pursed Lips

IT WAS Sunday morning. Ann and Barbara burst into their parents' room. The Sunday paper was strewn all over the bed. Ann and Barbara got into bed with Daddy and started to wrestle with him. Through the door that led to the bathroom, the new bathroom that they had added onto the house, they could see Mother's face in the mirror. She was putting on lipstick and her lips were pursed.

The Nest

ANN SAT ON THE FLOOR peeling an orange. After she had the peels off she gave them to Mommy. Mommy liked to eat the bitter white part just under the skin. Then Ann stuck her finger through the middle of the orange to open it. The juices ran in her mouth. Daddy called her to him and she sat on his lap. They were watching a good program on t.v. Daddy put his hand down her pants and patted her bottom. Some birds had made a nest in the corner fireplace and they began to chirp.

The Place Under the Ground

"TAGALONG," Barbara yelled at Ann as she and the other big kids started down the block. Ann started down the block the other way, skirting the place where the pavement bulged and running quickly past Mrs. Hathaway's house. Mrs. Hathaway was a witch. Now Ann was at the corner. She cut across the gas station over the tar black pavement with its wet pools of swirling colors to the vacant lot on the other side. The weeds grew high here, as tall as her waist. If she sat down here no one could see her. She sat down and watched the weeds growing thicker and thicker. Deeper in the lot the weeds grew even higher over a little mound, hiding the entrance to the underground place. The underground place was a secret. She could go there and no one would ever find her.

If She Loved Him
Shouldn't She Kiss Him?

ANN WAS INVITED into the living room. Nobody ever went into the living room. The fireplace had never been burned in there. The light was dim. The hibiscus bush outside the bay window and the heavy drapes obscured the light. Sometimes Ann came in here alone and moved around the room without touching the floor. She would go from the couch to the piano bench and from the piano bench to the yellow chair and from the yellow chair to the hassock. From the hassock she would move easily to the nubby chairs to the couch where she would lie back examining the people swarming in the picture overhead upside down.

Now strangers sat on the edge of the chairs. Ann was told that one of them was her uncle. Ann climbed up on his lap and gave him a kiss. Her uncle seemed to think that this was funny. She could tell from her parents' faces that she had not done the right thing. But if he was her uncle didn't she love him? And if she loved him shouldn't she kiss him?

The Tiny Islands

A TALL WOODEN FENCE made of vertical pointed boards
separated the driveway from the patio. Ann and Karen Rogers
stood on the crossbar peering over. Now it was a fort. Karen
Rogers was Annie Oakley and Ann was Lofty. Ann wanted
to be Annie Oakley but she was taller than Karen. She looked
up to Karen. Karen stood high on the fence and Ann stood
on the concrete. Her eyes were at a level with Karen's shins.
Karen's skin was brown and tan. The skin on her shin was
divided by tiny lines into tiny islands.

Ann Gets Barbara to
Take Her Medicine

BARBARA WAS SICK. The medicine would make her better but she did not want to take it. It was bitter. Ann was not sick. She poured out a spoonful of Barbara's medicine and opened her mouth. The medicine was bitter. She swallowed it. Only now would Barbara agree to take it.

Barbara Wishes Ann Good Night

ANN AND BARBARA lay in their beds on either side of the
room. "Good night," Barbara said. "Good night," Ann answered. "Good night," Barbara said again. "Good night," Ann
answered again. "Good night," Barbara repeated, demanding
an answer. "Good night," Ann said finally. All was now quiet.
Ann let out her breath. "Good night," Barbara said. Ann
clenched her fists in the dark. How could she leave this "good
night" unanswered? Could she go to sleep with this shutter
flapping open on one hinge? With one foot on the ground and
the other stepping off into a chasm? "Good night," Ann said.
There was no sound from Barbara's side of the room except
for Barbara's measured breathing. Ann lay very still waiting
for sleep. Her body began to tick off. "Good night," Barbara
said.

Ann Climbs a Tree

ANN LAY ON THE yellow chaise longue on the patio. She was reading a book. It was a story about a bunch of kids who have all sorts of exciting adventures together. Ann was alone. The sun was glaring through the late afternoon smog. She decided to climb a tree. It was an avocado tree with glossy smooth leaves. She hung from the first branch by her arms. Then she put her legs up and hung upside down. No one was there to see. She pulled herself up until she was sitting on the first bough. If someone had come into the yard they would have seen that she was the type of girl who liked to climb trees, but no one was there to see. She looked up at the next branch, but as soon as she tried to reach it she was afraid. She sat on the first branch dangling her legs. It looked like a long way down. No one came.

The Flood That Never Came

IT HAD BEEN RAINING. Big grey drops came down. But now it had cleared enough for them to go out on the playground for recess. Ann stood on the edge of a huge puddle in her red rain boots. In the puddle she saw the three stories of the brick school reflected. She saw the tall windows with their transoms above them. She saw the ledges and cornices and the place where the bird had hurled itself against the school and died. She saw the red white and blue flag and the pearly grey clouds moving above the roof. She stepped into the puddle. She waded out until the water almost reached the top of her boots. She wondered how deep the puddle was. Perhaps it was over her head. She hoped that it would rain some more. Then she would swim on the playground and people would come and go in boats.

Ann Stops

ANN COULDN'T WAIT for school to be over so that she could
stop at the corner store. There she bought two wax tubes full
of colored liquid and a small packet of sunflower seeds. She
bit off the tops of the tubes and sucked out the sweet juice
as she walked along. The street was straight and long. Big
leaves floated down in front of her. She was careful not to
step on any cracks. When there was a cement wall, she
walked up on the wall, placing one foot in front of the other,
and when she approached the corner where there was a light
she made her steps smaller and smaller if she saw the light
was red so that she would never have to stop until she was
home.

It was very quiet at home. Ann sat down on her bed and
opened a book. Then she opened her packet of sunflower
seeds and put several into her mouth, sucking the salt off.

She then began to crack them one by one, carefully removing the shells from her mouth and putting them in a pile on her nubby white bedspread. She parked the kernels under her lip until about four or five had accumulated. Then she removed them with her tongue, all along turning the pages, and relished them until they were gone. She lay down. She was in a narrow passage. It was dark, but the walls glowed red. The ceiling was so low that she had to crawl. Other passages went off to the left and right. The heat was suffocating. Ann woke up. She opened her eyes. Huge white nobs rose before her. They cast long shadows. There was a cool pool of spit under her mouth.

Their Pink Flesh

THE LITTLE GIRL across the street had a pink bedroom. In the pink bedroom was a four-poster bed with a pink canopy which matched the skirt of the vanity. It stood on a pink rug surrounded by pink walls.

Ann had brought her paper dolls. She had made them herself. They sat in the kitchen enclosed inside a nook. One paper doll was a man, the other was a woman. Gradually they are disrobed. Now you can see that they are quite well made with great attention to detail. They stand naked before us in their pink flesh.

Ann worries that the mother will think that what they are doing is dirty, so she is careful not to let her see what they are playing with. She knows the mother would not approve of the dolls because they are real. And they are real. Realer than us.

42

Sweet and Smooth and Salty

ANN WAS ON HER BIKE riding through the streets at dusk. She was following the paper boy. He didn't mind. He allowed her to follow him. She was not brave enough to ride through the streets alone. She would not know where she was going. But when she rode a few lengths behind the paper boy she had no fear. The wind whistled in her ear. The kerchief around her neck blew behind her. She was warm and the air was cold. When she returned home no one knew where she had been, least of all herself. She was hungry. In a drawer she found a fresh loaf of bread. She took a piece and buttered it. She did not usually butter her bread. She had not understood before why people buttered bread. But now it melted, sweet and smooth and salty, into her life.

The Statues

THE DARK GREEN LAWN slopes with the curvature of the
earth. The house is white behind it, behind the tall flower-
ing bush which obscures the window. The lawn is a thick
close cropped pad. Every so often there are little bare circles
enclosing a sprinkler head. They must be careful not to step
on these in their bare feet. "One, one hundred; two, one hundred; three, one hundred—" They move silently over the grass
while one alone covers her eyes. The sky is a deep dark blue.
There is the slightest chill in the air. Now the blind one
begins to move, her arms extended. All the others have
stopped, frozen in their tracks. They are statues; they will
always be there.

The Faces Reappear

ANN WATCHED the wallpaper. On it were red and rose and yellow flowers with green stems and leaves. The flowers bent and turned on a white field. They curled and receded backwards. The background came forward. White shapes that Ann had not seen before appeared. They formed themselves into faces and figures. Elegant ladies and hideous goblins peered out at her. But as she watched they faded backwards and the flowers came forward. She tried to force them back but they wouldn't come. She looked out the window. The light was fading. She turned back to the wall. There was a dark place on the wallpaper over the heater where she and Barbara stood as they dressed in the morning. Now the shapes in this dark place began to distinguish themselves. They bent their heads and turned towards her. The flowers tried to press forward, but she held them back, and she held the faces in her gaze until the darkness obliterated the room.

Objects in Plain Sight

ANN CAME INTO the den. There was a brick fireplace in one corner. Inside, birds had built a nest. The walls were knotty pine — warm, very busy, and full of knots. The rug was pea green. Ann often sat there peeling oranges. This was the room where everyone in the family spent most of their time. A couch faced the t.v. What else was there? There was a glass door leading to the new patio. Another led into the back porch which connected to the driveway and the kitchen. Another led into the hallway which connected the bedrooms and the front hall. It was through this door that Ann had come. While she had been out of the room Barbara had taken several every-day objects — ceramic figurines, vases, and the like — the sorts of things which ordinarily inhabited a room like this — and she had placed them in various places around the room — on the mantle, in the niche, on the end table, if there was an end table, etc. They were all in plain sight. Now Ann was searching for them. They were all in obvious places, but she was having difficulty finding them. They existed in a world which continued forever without interruption, and it was difficult for Ann to see them.

Life Through a Screen

ANN SAT on the floor with her face against the screen door watching the yard. The yard was divided into black squares which expanded as she looked. In these squares the lush foliage wavered in and out of focus. Tears melted the leaves. Some of the squares were atypical with rounded corners. Others were totally filled with blackness.

II. The Mother's Face

The Baby Is Up

ANN WAS TRYING to rock her baby to sleep in the carriage but her two-year-old was helping her.

Ties of Blood

ANN'S GREATEST FEAR, when she found out that her babies were going to be only twenty months apart, was that there would be jealousy between them. But why shouldn't they be friends? Actually, their closeness in age was an advantage. They could be playmates. Eventually. But then one day when Lena was just two and the baby, Molly, was only four months Abraham came to Ann with an astonished grin on his face. He had been watching the babies on the bed. "They were playing together!" he said. "They really were playing together!" Ann looked up at the baby he was holding on his arm. There was blood on her cheek.

Egg Break

As Ann unpacked the groceries Lena began to help. Each time Ann opened the refrigerator Lena lunged towards it grabbing whatever she could. Then Ann would say "No!" (nicely, cheerily), and try to put the next item away. She decided to try cooking dinner instead, abandoning the groceries on the table, half unpacked. Her casserole called for some canned corn. Canned corn! Canned corn! "I want some!" Lena said. Well, let me put you in your seat then, dear," Ann said (nicely, cheerily), picking Lena up and putting her in her seat. Then she put a little canned corn in a little bowl for Lena, hoping that would keep her occupied for a while while she cooked. Then she cooked and it was quiet, except for some quiet sizzling. The quiet was round, pure, whole. "Too quiet," Ann realized, turning to see the yellow mess in Lena's bowl of corn. It took her a few minutes to figure out what it was. Then she saw the egg carton she had left on the table. Lena had opened the carton and cracked the eggs very quietly.

No, Lena

"NO, LENA, draw on the *paper*, not on the wall. No, Lena, don't pee on the vacuum cleaner! Pee in your toilet. No, Lena, don't play in the toilet, the toilet is dirty. No, Lena, don't sit on the baby! Now the baby's crying. Give her a kiss. What a sweet sister! No, Lena, don't throw your food on the floor, please. No, Lena, we don't have any ice cream. Wouldn't you like a nice orange? What color is this, Lena? No-o, it's not blue. What color is it? Sunny and bright! It's yellow! Where are you going, darling? It's so quiet! Where are you, Lena? What are you doing? Lena, I'm afraid."

The Day Was Young

THE DAY was young. Ann was cleaning the soap off the bathroom wall. Lena had been playing with it the night before—mashing it on the wall and the shower curtain—while Ann was cleaning up the place where Lena had just accidentally peed on the rug while the baby screamed in the crib. The soap was foaming. Ann heard Lena padding down the hall. "Mommy!" Lena said, hugging Ann's leg. "I love you, Lena," Ann said.

The Sins of the Parents

ANN WENT IN to change the baby. She was thinking about the birthday card she had just received from her parents. It had been late. In it had been enclosed a small check. It had seemed very impersonal to Ann. She couldn't help but think that her parents had done this to make her feel bad. Suddenly she was aware that her own baby was crying. She had forgotten what she was doing. She looked down and smiled at the baby. The baby stopped crying and smiled back.

Waiting for Sleep

ANN WAS WAITING for Lena to fall asleep. They were lying in Lena's bed face to face. Lena put her finger on Ann's eyebrow. "And this is Mommy's eyebrow," she said. "Yes," Ann said. Lena put her finger on Ann's nose. "And this is Mommy's nose," she said. "Yes," Ann said. Lena put her finger on Ann's mouth. "And this is Mommy's mouth," she said. She put her finger in Ann's mouth and fingered her teeth. Then she explored Ann's ear, folding the lobe back and forth. "This is Mommy's ear," she said, tenderly. She was studying each feature of her mother intensely, minutely; she was committing her mother to memory. One day her mother would die.

For the Record

ANN LOOKED THROUGH the record collection trying to find one for children. She remembered someone had given them one sometime. She didn't have time to remember who what where. Lena was tearing the house apart brick by brick. It was called *Now We Are Six*. Ann put it on. Bang! Bang! Lena had unscrewed a lightbulb. Wasn't that clever? Ann's voice was bright and cheery. The world of make believe started to play. Christopher Robin had a nanny. Only, he called her Nan. Now she was sick.

They Play Together

ALL OF ANN'S underwear was strewn about the room. Lena had been playing with it. All of Ann's scarves were out of the drawer. Lena had been wearing them. All of the Kleenex was out of the box. Lena had pulled it out, piece by piece. Now the baby was chewing on it. "No, Baby!" Lena said, dancing over to smile into the baby's face. The baby began to laugh. Lena laughed back. The baby squealed. Ann's tears popped out. They really were playing together.

The Other Mother

LENA WAS IN THE STROLLER and the baby was on Ann's back. They walked into a boutique. Ann needed some new winter clothes. It had been years since she had bought any. Last winter she had been pregnant and the winter before that postpartum. Ann looked at the clothes wistfully, but she couldn't try them on with the babies along. She turned awkwardly and started to push the stroller out of the store. "Hey!" a voice shouted. "I've got two, too!" Ann looked up to see who she had jostled. There was a woman pushing a baby in a stroller with a toddler walking beside. She was tired looking and dressed in clothes several years out of style. Ann hated this woman instantly.

Why This Happened

THE BABY WAS ASLEEP. Ann was cuddling Lena on her bed, hoping she would nap, now, too. Then she would have some time alone. She thought about all the things she wanted to do. The possibilities were limitless. Lena's eyes closed. The tension began to leave her body. Ann poised, ready to leap from the little bed. Then she heard the baby waking up. Were they in cahoots? One ready to come on duty just as the other went off? Ann wondered why this was happening to her. She picked the baby up, changed her and nursed her. But the baby was still crying. She cried louder and louder. Ann examined her. Her two front teeth looked ready to break through the gum. She was in pain. She needed Ann to hold her and rock her. Ann was grateful Lena was sleeping. Molly needed her whole attention. That was why this had happened.

The Mother's Face

"READ!" LENA SAID. Ann and Lena were lying in Lena's bed. Ann read her a story. "This is my night-night," Lena said, cuddling her blanket around her. Ann cuddled Lena in her night-night. The night-night was a quilt Ann had made for her before she was born. It was very primitive because Ann didn't sew very well, but Ann had wanted to make something for her baby and it delighted her that Lena was attached to it. "Here!" Lena said, handing Ann her bottle and turning over on her back. "She really seems to be falling asleep," Ann thought. It was an hour earlier than usual. The baby, also, was already asleep. Ann was delighted. She would have an hour to herself before going to bed. She smiled down at the angel sleeping in her arms. Lena's eyes fluttered open for a moment. In that moment she absorbed the shining face of the mother shining down on her with love. It would be there forever.

Permission to Sing

IT WAS RAINING, so Ann sang a song about the rain for Lena and Molly: "It's raining, it's pouring, the old man is snoring; he went to bed and he bumped his head and he couldn't get up in the morning." This reminded her of another song and she sang that one: "Rain, rain, go away, come again another day, my girls and I want to go out and play in the rain, rain, go away—" The third song made her feel like dancing: "I'm singing in the rain, just singing in the rain, what a wonderful feeling, I'm happy again, I walk down the lane, with a hap-pap-pappy refrain, I'm singing, just singing in the rain. Let the stormy clouds chase, everyone from the place, come on with the rain, I've a smile on my—" Ann was singing and dancing all around the room. The children watched and wiggled to the music. To them it was perfectly natural. They did not see a thirty-seven year old woman cavorting in her apartment.

Learning Patience

ANN HAD BEEN WITH the children all day. Now the baby was asleep and it was time for Lena to go down, but she was overtired and unruly. Ann felt she didn't have the patience to deal with her anymore. Abraham went in armed with a fresh bottle to lie down with her. Then Ann escaped to her own room where she lay down alone at last with a book. It was a book of art from the Nazi concentration camps—a gift from her sister. Ann couldn't bear to look at any pictures or read anything about the holocaust. She began to leaf through the book. How could it be? These stick figures—these children tortured in front of their parents. There was no way to reconcile this. Abraham came into the room. "I can't take anymore," he said. "She won't go to sleep! She keeps asking for you."

Ann leapt up and ran down the hall to Lena's bed, and there she lay with her, kissing her and petting her until she was asleep. Millions of children had died horrible deaths, and this was all she could do to help.

Reacquainted

IT WAS NOW eight o'clock, and Lena had been without a nap all day. Suddenly she was in her bed, sucking on a bottle. Her eyes were closed. She was asleep. Ann couldn't believe this had happened. She hadn't been to sleep this early for five months. Never before ten. Usually eleven. Ann was terrified. Would she waken in an hour and be up for the rest of the night? Perhaps it was late enough, perhaps she would sleep through the night. Ann played with the baby. Soon the baby, too, was asleep. A vast evening full of infinite possibilities stretched before Ann. She began to reacquaint herself with herself. Soon she began to think about her figure and her career. She compared them to other people's figures and careers. She suddenly felt lonely. Was she lonely? She read a book, luxuriating in that possibility. It was charming, amusing. But did it matter? Was it important? By now it was almost midnight. Suddenly, Ann heard a cry. Lena was awake, calling for her. Ann bolted from her bed and ran down the hall. "Mommy is here," she said. Lena was crying. "Do you want a bottle?" Ann asked. "I want a bottle milk," Lena said. Her eyes were not open. Ann ran to the kitchen and brought the bottle back. She brought it to Lena. Lena began to suck. Ann held her. "Mommy loves Lena," Ann said. "You are Mommy's cuddle-puss," she said, cuddling her. Lena handed Ann the bottle. She was asleep again. Ann looked down at her. She was lying on her belly. One bare shoulder could be glimpsed where the nightgown opened. It was the most tender, most beautiful thing Ann had ever seen.

Ann Steps Down

WHEN ANN WALKED ALONG with Lena and Molly and encountered the gaze of strangers, she did not hope, as once she had, that she would see in their gaze admiration for her own person. Now she was looking for them to notice the beauty of her children. "I step aside," she said, surprised that she wanted to, surprised at how ready she was to put her children ahead of herself as they walked under the sky and through the dark. The baby cried out in the night and Ann hurried from her bed and stumbled down the long dark hall, pulling her robe about her. The baby was standing in the crib, the tears streaming from her face. Ann picked her up and began to comfort her, She was getting heavy. Ann walked in the hall. The baby was getting heavier and heavier, but the tears had dried on her face. The wooden floor was hard under Ann's feet. The baby was now so heavy that Ann found she was having trouble walking. She was being pressed into the floor.

Ann Fills With Hate

"DO SOMETHING! Do something!" Ann screamed to Abraham. "There's nothing to do. Don't worry, she'll be fine. It won't hurt her a bit," he said. Lena had just downed a small glass of wine. It had happened while Ann was washing the dishes. Their dinner guest had been clearing the table. She seemed nice enough — intelligent and pleasant. Ann had remembered seeing the glass quite full of wine on the dining room table before she had left the room. This woman had been bringing the dishes in and stacking them on the kitchen table behind Ann so that when Ann turned she saw Lena just setting the empty glass back down on the table. Now she would be drunk, sick, or become an alcoholic. This woman had no children and did not consider that Lena would be able to or was likely to reach for anything on the kitchen table.

Had she been a mother, she would probably have poured the wine out as soon as she brought it into the kitchen. But she was not child-conscious. Therefore, Ann hated her.

Still Life

THE LIGHT SHONE IN through the lace curtain and a pattern of brightness and shadow appeared on the umbrella stroller and on the blue couch and baby-sized doll and doll blanket Lena had placed there. The doll's fingers were splayed as if she were fending something off—perhaps the brightness which illuminated each finger. Her eyes were turned toward the couch cushion. She looked like she had a question, and it was not resolved. Behind her—the work of many thoughtful hours—a multicolored afghan was displayed. The quiet in the room was intense. Both babies were asleep, their merry eyes shut, their sweet pink mouths relaxed against the afternoon, their bubbling persons stilled, surrendered to dreams and the arcing of the light as afternoon passed into night.

What She Longed For

"MUSIC, PWEESE," Lena begged, so Ann put on a record so that Lena could dance. It was one Ann had not listened to for a long time. Now it brought back a flood of memories of the time before Ann had met Abraham. Suddenly, she was filled with longing, remembering herself dancing alone to this music, the fire burning and her skirts twirling. She remembered turning the volume up on the radio while she drove with all the windows down at sixty miles per hour over windy lonely roads to the ocean, this music filling the car and the world with longing like waves rolling and rolling against the shore. And what was all this longing for? Ann looked at Lena dancing naked on the floor and the baby sitting, smiling, her hands clasped together, and Abraham just coming in the door.

Ann Yells at Abraham

In Ann's other life, before she had met Abraham and before Lena and Molly were born, Ann had subscribed to the idea that the only way to have a perfect marriage was not to have children. In that way one could devote all of one's energy to perfecting the relationship. Needless to say, that relationship was sterile.

When Ann and Abraham had met, they had decided to have children immediately. Ann had become pregnant with Lena on their wedding night. Ann and Abraham had had love at first sight and had felt their relationship was perfect from the first moment. But when Lena was born that feeling of perfection had doubled. Now, with Molly along, their relationship seemed triply perfect. They all loved each other unconditionally and they lived together in utter harmony. Ann had never been angry at Abraham for one moment. Then, one night, he left the aspirin bottle where Lena could reach it.

The Figure

ANN WAS PUSHING the babies in the double stroller through the joggers in the park. It seemed that everyone in the world was doing some sort of exercise. Before Lena was born Ann herself had used to swim three quarters of a mile each day. Afterwards, it was more difficult for Ann to leave the house, so she had taken up the exercycle. She was able to ride five miles a day while Lena napped. But now that Molly had joined them Ann found that she was unable to even manage that. But, on the other hand, now she didn't seem to need it. Her figure, miraculously, was better than it had ever been. She got more than enough exercise, it seemed, simply carrying the babies around and picking up toys all day. She was always ravenously hungry, and she consumed more cake and bread than she had heretofore in her lifetime, but still she continued to grow thinner. Perhaps it was the enormous number of calories it took to breast feed the baby that allowed Ann to eat so much junk with impunity. Perhaps it was not ever sleeping a night through that required so much extra energy or perhaps she simply burnt calories at an accelerated rate every time Molly fell over or Lena pulled the curtains down on their heads or she heard a scream in the middle of the night.

Ann lifted Lena out of the stroller and lifted it with Molly up the stairs and into their building. She put the stroller down and, holding Lena's hand, pushed the stroller with Molly crying now to the elevator. "So much for the myth that childbearing ruins your figure," she thought to herself as she negotiated the children out of the elevator and into the door. There was a smug smile on her face as she passed by the mirror. The face she glimpsed there looked to be about one hundred eighty-seven years old.

Her Own Medicine

ANN WAS DEPRESSED, but she didn't know why. It was a vague feeling. She was trying to express it to Abraham in the kitchen when she started to cry. Lena was sitting naked on the kitchen table and Molly was escaping down the hall. Abraham went to chase the baby and Ann found Lena was feeding her with a tiny toy spoon. "Daddy's getting the baby," Lena said to her. "You feel better? You feel better." Lena kissed her. "You feel better, Mommy," Lena said. Ann had to feel better. She was being given a dose of her own medicine.

Life and Order

THE CHILDREN scattered their toys around the room while Ann picked them up and organized them while the children scattered them around the room. Ann was bored. She took the children into another room. There the children pulled books from the shelves while Ann picked them up and put them back while they pulled the books from the shelves. After the children were asleep Ann would be able to put every single one back. But they would never be just they way they were. There would be a new torn dust-jacket. Ann pulled a corner of a page from the baby's mouth. Some words, important to someone once: now they were mush. Ann's nerves felt thin and brittle. In this world, everything tended towards chaos and decay. The baby screamed a complaint. Ann picked her up and they followed Lena into a third room. Lena was pouring imaginary tea into red and yellow and blue cups.

"Here's your tea, King," Lena said, handing the blue cup to Ann. "Thank you," Ann said. "Here's some for you, Pwince," Lena said, handing the red cup to Baby. Baby began to drink, and, as if by magic, the world changed direction and tended towards life and order.

The End of Days

ANN LOOKED AT the children. Lena was standing on the huge dictionary which Abraham had left on the bed. "Here's Lena!" Lena said, her hands upraised. The baby was climbing onto a box on the floor. Now she was standing up! She was raising her hands. She was laughing, delighted at her own prowess and daring and skill. It seemed to Ann that neither of them ever stopped moving. They never stopped striving upward, forward. What was it that drove them, that propelled them? Soon Lena would no longer be a toddler, she would be a child. Then Molly would be a toddler, not a baby. Something had been pushing them along from the moment they were born, since before they were born. What was it that hurled them along so joyfully to the end of days?

Where Time Goes

ANN SAT in the big white wicker rocker looking out the window. The baby was standing in the playpen, chortling. Outside in the deep blue evening people were hurrying home from work. Ann and the babies had not been outside all day. Where had the day gone? What had happened? As usual, the girls had taken a bath together with cups and boats and sieves and splashing and laughing. There had been lunch—on the floor and in the air. And naps. How Ann had held those golden curly heads to her breast! How many kisses were there in that day? That day when nothing had happened. Oh, there had been a game of ball in the hall—a game they always played—and the baby had waved bye-bye over and over. Ann marveled that she felt so peaceful, that she didn't feel restless. Down below in the world the cars swished over the wet streets. People were rushing from here to there. They were all trying to get home. "Mommy," a voice said. Ann looked up. Another cherub had appeared in the room.

The Cow Was in the Hall

"I'M SCARED," Lena said. There was a cow in the hall. Ann took her hand. She tried to show her that it was only Daddy's overcoat draped across the stroller. "I'm scared," Lena said. "It's dark. The dark hurts me." Ann wished she had a ladder so she could replace the hall light. Then she would prove to Lena that there was nothing there. "Don't worry," Ann said. "Mommy is here. Mommy won't let anything hurt you. Shall I read you a story?" "Neeyeah," Lena said. It was her way of saying "yes" without compromising herself and melting into her mother. She was her own person, separate from her mother. A long dark hall separated her room from her mother's room. No longer was she a little monkey; she was a person. She could hold in her pee and hold her temper. The animal had been banished. It had gone to live in the hall.

Ann Reads a Story;
Lena Hears a Story

LENA ASKED ANN to read her a story. It was her favorite. She had Ann read it to her again and again. She even acted it out with Baby. So Ann knew it was the story of her life. It was about a boy who had to leave his mother and go on a quest. He had to face many dangers and endure many trials. At last, he was transformed and filled with power. Ann deduced that through this story Lena was teaching herself that in order to find herself she would have to separate from her mother. Why was that necessarily so? Ann wondered. Lena was teaching herself also, Ann could see, that only through suffering could she gain power and wisdom and find fulfillment. But Ann did not want Lena to suffer. She was going to prevent it at all costs.

Down on the Floor

ANN LAY on the floor like a mother lion, her cubs climbing all over her. Her expression was impassive. Only the switch of her tail indicated the violence she contained. The cubs swatted at each other, falling, laughing, crying, screaming. The mother lion tolerated all this by remaining a million miles away. "Talk! Talk!" Lena called at her face. "Oh, hello!" Ann said. "Aren't we having a nice time?"

Something Larger

THEY SPENT minute after minute, hour after hour, year after year taking care of their children. Their children began helpless and needed everything done for them, but gradually they grew older and more self-reliant. Then they needed them less and less. Meanwhile, their parents had been growing older. Then their parents needed a little help, and then more and more. So they began to take care of their parents. They were tall and strong. Their energy was boundless. Then they themselves began to age. They didn't know what to make of it. They had always taken care of everybody else, now they needed someone to take care of them. They didn't want to admit it, they denied it. They didn't want to give in. But it didn't matter. Their children came to them and gathered round them. And finally they had to surrender. There was another presence in the room. Something larger.

A Comparison

ANN WAS WORRIED about Lena. At night, as soon as she was put in bed, she asked to get up and pee. Then she would sit on the toilet but no pee would come. As soon as she was put back in bed she would ask to pee again. Ann knew this was a delaying tactic. She did not want to go to sleep. Perhaps she was afraid of nightmares. Or perhaps she was afraid of the inevitable — that she would wake up in the middle of the night and have to pee. Or perhaps she was afraid of the unthinkable — that she would wet the bed. Whatever the cause, Ann was worried. Did she have a disturbed child? "Oh, they all do that," her sister-in-law reassured her. Ann was greatly relieved. Her child was normal.

The phone rang. It was their friend Don. He had just gotten back from Washington D.C. where he had been visiting his little niece who was only three weeks younger than

Molly. He was very excited because she was standing on her own now. "Oh, Molly's been doing that for quite a while," Ann said. He was very impressed because his niece had actually said a few words. "Molly waves and says bye-bye!" Ann said. "That's just what my niece says," Don said. "Bye-bye!" "Isn't that wonderful?" Ann said. But she was not sincere. She was too polite, however, to tell Don that whereas her baby might say the same word as his niece that did not indicate that they were in any way alike.

Ann Was a Child

ANN WAS SITTING on Lena's bed watching her play on the floor with her dolls' house. She was putting tiny people into tiny chairs. The tiny people were talking to one another. They were offering each other dinner and telling each other to go to bed. Now they were being put into tiny beds.

Baby Molly was sitting in the opposite corner babbling happily into her pop-up telephone. She was in the middle of a very important conversation. The clear sunlight slanted in through the window the way it does in childhood.

The world was flush with itself. Ann was as absorbed in that happy present reality as were the other two. Only, for her, the memory of that feeling was also present.

The Plot

SOME PEOPLE felt sorry for Ann because she spent most of her time with the children. She rarely talked with anyone over three. She did not often get to have a really adult conversation. Sometimes, however, when she was out doing her errands she would overhear adults talking. It was usually about the plots of t.v. shows.

The Stupid Parents

ANN AND ABRAHAM were telling their friend Lenore a tale
of woe. It had been months since Lena had gone to sleep at
a decent hour. It was never before ten, and if she happened
to take her nap after three in the afternoon, it was usually
eleven or later. They always tried to put her down early but
rarely had any success. "We never had any trouble getting
Harvey to bed," Lenore said. "He always went to bed early.
Of course, he gave up his nap at about two and a half." Lena
was now two and a half, Ann realized. The next day, Ann
did not try to put her down to nap at all. It was a relief not
to be involved in that struggle. At about five in the afternoon
Lena began to look like she was going to sleep, but Abraham
was able to tickle her awake again. That night both children
were asleep by eight-thirty. There had been no bedtime bat-
tle. Ann and Abraham looked at each other. They had the

whole rest of the evening to talk — like couples do in the evening. Was life going to be normal now, just like that? After all their struggling was the solution going to be so simple? Could Lena have given up her nap months ago? Ann and Abraham sat peacefully on the couch feeling stupid.

Some Uses of Memory

ANN WAS READING Lena a book. In the book there was a picture of a child riding a horse. Suddenly Ann remembered a time when she was a child and she rode a horse. There was the sagebrush and the horse and the blue sky and the dust. Ann felt a pang. Where was that day, that ride, that child now? Gone forever? Where was her life, all the little pieces of it? Scattered—dissolved—hidden! A feeling of mourning overcame her. "Do you remember when I was a little baby and I used to tear books?" Lena asked. "I don't remember that," Ann said. "Do you remember when I was a baby and Baby was a Lena?" Lena asked. "No, darling," Ann said. "I don't remember that." She had to smile. Obviously Lena thought you could do whatever you pleased with memory.

Free Time

LENA AND MOLLY had been going to bed early for over a week now. Every night they had dinner at six-thirty and every night they had a bath at seven. Every night they were in their beds by seven-thirty and every night they were asleep by eight. It was now a routine, a pattern, a habit. It was a puzzle where all the pieces fit. And inside the pattern Ann was happy, knowing she had something to rely on and knowing she had the whole rest of the evening to herself. At last the children were asleep. The rest of the evening stretched before her, formless and horrible.

It's Hard to Believe

IT WAS OBVIOUS to everyone in the world that Ann was the mother of Molly and Lena. Wherever they went, people knew that she was named "Mommy." Strangers would bend down, for example, to tell Lena and Molly that they looked just like "Mommy." They were referring to Ann. Other times, friends would try to pick Lena up, but she would cry, "I want my mommy!" and turn, her eyes worried, searching for Ann. Everyone knew Ann was a mommy, but Ann had only been a mommy for two and a half years. Before she had been a mommy she had, presumably, been something else that had, presumably, its own reality. Molly called out "Mama!" and she cried until Ann picked her up. Then she put her little arms around Ann's neck and hugged her the way children hug their mothers—with a passionate fear that they might disappear.

100

The Bubble Bursts

ANN SAT on the bed watching Lena turning on the rug before her. Lena was dancing her perpetual dance of life and Ann reached out her arms to catch her and kiss her. But Lena eluded her and continued to dance. Lena's eyes were so bright and her curls were so curly — Ann just wanted to capture her for one moment, but she twirled away and away and away. Lena was naked and pink, a bright flower Ann was trying to pluck, but she twirled away from Ann, and out of her backside popped a small stinky bubble.

The Children Are Pushed Out

LENA HAD THREE beautiful books by Robert McClosky. In
the first, *Blueberries for Sal*, Sal was a little girl even younger
than Lena. She didn't have a baby sister yet. She was alone
with her mommy on an adventure. In the second book, *One
Morning in Maine*, she was older. Now she had a baby sister,
just like Lena had. Ann found this of great interest. "You're
like Sal, and Baby's like Sal's baby sister, Jane!" Ann said to
Lena. "I'm Lena!" Lena insisted. In the next book, *Time of
Wonder*, both Jane and Sal were quite a bit older. They were
girls now, not babies. They didn't toddle after their mother,
they swam and explored on their own. "See, that's Jane and
that's Sal," Ann said, pointing them out to Lena. "Only, they're
older in this book," Ann said. She was cuddling Lena in her
lap. Molly was playing at her feet. Ann looked at the
copyright of the book. Sal, or the child Sal was modeled after,

must be about her own age now, she realized. Tears rose to Ann's eyes. Where had her childhood gone? Lena, in the meantime, had been growing impatient. Suddenly, she pushed the books away. Then the children who were there in the room came forward and the ones who were not were pushed out.

Parade at the Dinner Table

WHEN THE BABYSITTER let them in the door Ann and Abraham and their dinner guests found Lena and Molly all dressed up in scarves. Baby Molly had one trailing behind her like a cape. Lena had on several layers, so that she looked ready to do a dance of seven veils. They were dancing and laughing down the hall in what they called a parade. Abraham took Lena and Ann took Molly and they each put a girl to bed. Then they sat down to dine in a civilized fashion with their guests. Ann sat composedly at the table while the food was being passed and the people talked. The candles burned and reflected in the wine glasses. Ann sat there but she wasn't really there. She was in the parade, following her children down the hall once again.

The Most Beautiful Girl

BEFORE BABY MOLLY was born Ann and Abraham were in the habit of telling Lena that she was the most beautiful girl in the world. She was Mommy's most wonderful girl, the world's smartest girl, the most adorable girl in the world, etc. But now that Molly was here, how could they talk that way? Now Ann tried to remember to say "Mommy's most beautiful *big* girl," or "one of the *two* most beautiful girls in the world." Ann tried to say this, but it was too awkward. So, at last, she went back to telling Lena that she was the most beautiful girl. But now she also told Molly that *she* was the most beautiful girl in the world.

The Judgement

Ann was thinking about her past life, considering each event. She was incredulous. Could she be the very same person who had done such horrid things? How could her behavior have been so misguided? She cringed as she remembered certain details. She wished she could hide, but she couldn't hide from herself. She couldn't understand why happiness had been granted to her now after the life she had led. Her husband and her daughters gave her such joy that she often felt that it would be all right at last to die. She filled with a feeling of terrible sadness, almost of mourning, for the person who didn't deserve any of this.

Ice Cream and Sand

SUNDAY IN THE PARK. Abraham helps Lena climb to the very top of the jungle gym. Ann looks up from the sandbox where she and Molly are making cakes. Other parents sit on benches. There is a dreamy look on the children's faces. The sun shines. Great leafy trees march up and down. An ice cream truck pulls up. Everyone can have some, no one is denied.

A couple walk by pushing a long carriage. In the carriage sleep three babies — triplets! Ann wonders how it is for these people. It is so intense for her and Abraham just having two. The couple look strangely peaceful. They are holding hands. Abraham has noticed them also. His arm steals around Ann. They smile at each other. Then Lena and Molly come over and hug their legs. Their little fingers are sticky. Abraham holds Ann, and their children bind them with ice cream and sand.

107

The Longing to Be Touched

ANN WAS SITTING on the floor in Lena's room. Molly toddled over from across the room and turning carefully sat down with a deliberate plop into Ann's lap. Lena was pressing her naked belly into Ann's back while she worked on Ann's hair mercilessly—alternately with a small brush and her bristle blocks. "Gently, gently!" Ann begged. "Does that hurt? That doesn't hurt," Lena said, melodically, as if saying it in this phony voice made it undeniable. It was the very same cheerful voice Ann always used with Lena when she wished to have her way with her, Ann realized. The truth was that she loved to have Lena playing with her hair though she pulled it and made it into an utter tangled mess. It felt good to have Molly's solid form squarely placed on top of hers. The truth was Ann could never get enough of this pure physical closeness with these bodies that had come out of her body.

An image played before her on the color t.v. which had been on all along in the foreground. It was an ad for blue jeans. It was the news of the world up to that minute. A backside in blue jeans longing to be touched.

Thank God

ABRAHAM WAS HOLDING Lena on his lap. She was fresh from her bath and dressed in her pink nightgown with rosebuds. Her mouth was a rosebud. She smiled up at her father adoringly then hugged him around the neck. "I love you, Daddy," she said. Her little arms held him tightly. "I love you, Lena," Abraham said, holding her tenderly. His eyes were closed. He was talking to God.

Just Grace

Ann and Lena and Molly were finally dressed and ready to go out. "Do you want to go to the health food store?" Ann asked. It was a stupid question. "I want to go to the park!" Lena said. Molly bounced affirmatively in the stroller. "Do you want to walk or ride?" Ann asked. "I want to run!" Lena said. "Hold on to the stroller while we cross the street," Ann said.

Molly was holding onto a book and peering at it intently as they rolled along, like a person reading in the subway. Yet there were trees and dogs and children riding tiny motorcycles passing them in both directions. Pigeons fluttered up and up and up as they passed. Molly dropped the book. As Ann reached down to get it, Molly reached out to her. But it was a bit early for her bribe.

Ann liked to reserve the bribe for the walk home when

Molly might have sand in her diaper and not want to sit down or be overripe for her nap and want to kick, but she reached into her pack and pulled out a graham cracker. Now Lena was jumping: "*I* want one!" but Ann had anticipated this and was already offering her the first piece—she was the first born—and now here was Molly's. Molly pushed hers away. Now Ann understood that Molly wanted to get out of the stroller to walk like her big sister.

Now that she was walking she deigned to accept a cookie.

At first this cookie was a problem because it was in two pieces—a little piece in her right hand and a big piece in her left. These cookies prevented her from holding her mommy's hand, and so all three of them had to remain at a standstill while Molly ate the little cookie and transferred the big cookie to her other hand—just in time, for Lena was growing impatient. Now they were able to travel the last fifty feet to the playground.

When they got there there was only one baby there already with his father. He had been bribed with cheese crackers. He offered one to Lena and she gave him a graham cracker. Then Molly went over to him with the remains of her cookie and gave it to him. "Sometimes I think this is more of a smorgasbord than a playground," Ann remarked to the father.

"We had resolved never to let little David eat between-meal snacks, but toddlers seem to eat all the time," the man remarked. He was a brutish looking fellow, a type of man Ann found particularly repugnant. The park made for strange bedfellows. There were no other people there and hence, no escape. The man was now at liberty, nay, compelled, to tell Ann about his son's sleeping habits.

Little David had not taken a nap on Saturday and yet had not gone to bed until ten. Ann had no pity for him. After all, she had two children. "But two are a lot easier," the man insisted. "They amuse each other. No! David! Don't be a bad boy! Do you want me to take you home?" Little David was

112

pouring sand on the head of another little child who had just arrived.

Lena had started to run laps around the sandbox and Molly was toddling after her. Now she was falling into a hole. Ann raced to pick her up. "Let's go in the sandbox," she suggested. Lena was already in there making a cake. Another mother had come with her daughter. She and her daughter looked just alike. They both had round faces and lank hair pulled back into ponytails. There was nothing pretty about the woman, but her face, as she proudly and lovingly watched her daughter playing in the sand, was beautiful nonetheless.

Now the horrible father of little David was joining them in the sand. Little David had come to dig next to Lena and Molly. Little David and his father also looked just alike. Little David was now offering Lena one of his sand toys. His father beamed down on him lovingly. Just for that moment he seemed to Ann to be transformed into something glorious. She was surprised.

But now it was time to get Lena and Molly back in the carriage. If they didn't leave now they wouldn't be home in time to take their naps. Usually they didn't want to leave the park to go home to take naps. But today they went quite willingly. Ann didn't know why. She didn't even need the bribe she had held in reserve — raisins — but she offered it to them anyway. Perhaps it was because they had arisen so early in the morning. Or perhaps there was no explanation — it was just grace.

On the Platform

ANN, ABRAHAM, LENA AND MOLLY were standing on the crowded subway platform waiting for a train. Suddenly a man without shoes or shirt appeared in front of them. He was staring at Lena. "I have never seen such a beautiful girl!" he said. Ann and Abraham started to sweat. Lena was eating raisins. He reached his hand out for her to pour some in and she did. Ann held tight to Lena's other hand. "I don't suppose you could go away with me?" the man suggested to Lena. Ann and Abraham tried to laugh. Some of Lena's raisins had fallen on the platform. The man bent over and picked them up. Lena stared at him. He was pretending to eat them. "You are the most beautiful girl I have ever seen," the man repeated, "but now I must catch my train." He disappeared up the stairs. Ann and Abraham began to breath again. Later they compared notes: They had each discovered that it is terrifying to be a parent of girls. And they had each wondered why the man hadn't noticed that Molly was equally beautiful.

Happy Day

ANN WAS WALKING the children through the park to school. Molly, in the front seat of the stroller, was reaching down to touch the tops of the late summer weeds that lined the path. Lena, who was helping Ann to push her, was looking at the first autumn leaves which had started to drift down. Ann wondered if she remembered last autumn's leaves or if this year would be the first she would remember. They all looked up as a flock of pigeons rose before them and fluttered deeper into the tunnel of tall shimmering trees through which they were hurrying. "Look!" Lena said. "There are flowers in the tree!" Ann looked, but she didn't see any flowers, only a dazzle of light as the wind pushed the leaves high up against the perfect blue heavens. Perhaps this was the first day of the creation of the world. Molly, who had been humming a little tune, now began to sing a song with only one word: "hap-py, hap-py, hap-py."

All Alone

ANN WAS ALONE in the house with the children. The windows were all closed because a chill had begun to set into the world. The day outside was grey, opaque. Occasionally some street noises would drift up—jackhammers and other random bits of chaos. And then it was quiet. The children climbed onto the breakfast table and Ann removed them. The phone rang. It was an acquaintance of Ann's, the mother of a two-year-old. She wondered if Ann knew of a good babysitter.

Ann did not. She felt a little resentful of this woman who had called not because she wanted to be friends with Ann but because she was looking for someone to take her child off her hands. Lena and Molly were sitting on the breakfast table again.

Ann wondered what she would be doing now if she didn't

have Lena and Molly. Perhaps she would be having coffee with a friend, sharing her feelings. "You have to get off the table now so we can have eggy, girls," she said. Probably she would be back at work, back in the "real world" busily engrossed in the affairs of adults. Most women these days, she knew, went right back to work and put their children in daycare. They were terrified, perhaps, of the isolation of motherhood. They didn't want to be closed into this kitchen where children were in imminent danger of falling off the table. It was, according to an article in the Sunday paper, an unnatural situation for a mother to be home alone with her children. Perhaps this isolation Ann was feeling was unnatural, but it was nonetheless real. But would it be any more natural for her to be out in the world covering it up?

A Bunny Runs Away

ANN AND LENA were lying in Lena's bed reading stories. Ann was reading Lena about the runaway bunny. No matter how far away the bunny went the mommy bunny would always come and catch her and hold her in her arms. Ann held Lena in her arms and Lena put her arms around Ann's neck and hugged her back. Ann looked down on Lena lovingly. She had never seen such a beautiful vibrant creature. "Now it's time to get cozy and go to sleep," Ann said. "So that we can wake up in the morning and go to school?" Lena asked. "Yes," Ann said. She was happy that Lena loved school, that she was looking forward to it. This was just the beginning, Ann knew. From now on Lena would want and need to be away from her more and more until she was finally launched into her own life. "But no matter how far you go, I will always be ready to catch you in my arms and hug you, my little bunny," Ann said. She was very happy that Lena loved school so well. "Let go, you're squeezing me," Lena said.

Playing Herself

EVERY DAY before Lena took her nap Ann would read her a story. The story she always wanted to hear of late was "Jack and the Beanstalk." Ann wondered why it was so important to her right now. She wondered if it had anything to do with the fact that the father in the story was dead and the father figure in the story never came home until the mother figure had fed the child and he was tucked away. Abraham had been working very late lately. Lena had been getting up more in the night and coming into their bed or dragging Abraham off to hers. Perhaps it was only the Oedipal stage. Lena was only three, but already she had a complicated psychology. Molly, however, did not seem to have much of a psychology at all, yet. She said "Hum-ty!" when she wanted her Humpty Dumpty doll. She said "Nigh!" when Ann put her in the crib at night. But sometimes, when Lena was frustrated about something and would start to cry, Molly would start to cry. Was it sympathy, Ann wondered, or simple imitation? One day when Ann tried to brush Lena's hair and Lena turned on her to scratch her Molly raced over to scratch Ann also. Did she think it was a game? Molly was like an actress in a play— she was just playing herself until she had one.

Understanding

MOLLY AND LENA were now going to school three hours a day and they both seemed to love it. Moreover, it had regularized their schedules for the first time so that they were now getting up at the same time every morning, taking naps at the same time every afternoon, and going to bed at the same time every night. For a while, Ann had tried to get Lena to give up her nap, but that had proved a disaster, as she either got impossibly wild in the evening or took a very late nap despite all of Ann and Abraham's efforts to keep her up, and then she would be up all night. But now at last it seemed Ann and Abraham were really on top of the problem. The girls woke automatically at 7:30 a.m. They went to the park from 10 to 11:30. Molly was popped back into her crib promptly at noon. Then Ann read stories to Lena until 12:30 when Lena took her nap. At 1:30 they were awakened, popped into their double stroller and pushed to school where together Ann and Abraham collected them at 5:00. So much of their energy was sapped at school that by 9:00 Molly was ready to be popped back into her crib where she pulled the covers over her head and said "Nigh!" Lena was then allowed one more hour of stories, and then Abraham would be called in to put the crowning touch on the day's schedule. He would have her asleep by 10:00.

Molly really loved school and Ann loved the benefit of having a daily routine established at last. Now she was usually asleep by 11:00. Now she was usually awake by midnight.

Molly was calling her. She was bellowing "Ma-meeeee!" Ann went down the hall to nurse her and change her and put her to sleep again. Then Ann went back to sleep.

"Ma-meeee! Ma-meee!" Molly was calling again. Ann checked her watch. It was only 2:00 a.m. Suddenly Ann noticed that this had been going on for days. Molly was waking up every two hours. Ann was getting up with her four times a night. The first night Ann was sure it was a fluke. But after five nights, Ann wondered if it wasn't now an impossibly ingrained habit.

She opened Molly's mouth to look at her teeth. She had overheard another mother in the park explain her son's temper tantrum by the fact of his teething. Sure enough, here were some teeth just poking through. But somehow Ann didn't think it was teething that was bothering Molly in the night. When Ann entered her room she seemed perfectly happy. She didn't seem to be in pain.

Then it dawned on Ann that Molly was checking on her. Making sure she was still there. Ann now had three consecutive hours to do whatever she pleased. She wondered if she should use them to get three consecutive hours of sleep.

Well, perhaps, she reasoned, when Molly understands that no matter how many times I go away I always come back

125

she will let me sleep a little more. If, indeed, that is the explanation.

She had noticed that most of the discussions amongst the mothers in the park centered on the explanations for whatever behavior patterns their children were displaying. Even Lena, lately, had begun to show an interest in explanations. She liked to give explanations. "Because it is Thursday," she would say. Needless to say, it was Tuesday, and the day of the week had nothing to do with what she was trying to explain. But she would nod her head up and down affirming her position. Like Ann and all the mothers in the park, she was fond of understanding.

How Little

Aɴɴ ᴡᴀs ᴡᴀʟᴋɪɴɢ Lena home from school. It was Friday, the day Molly stayed home, so it was just the two of them. With one hand, Lena was holding a box of animal crackers and with the other she held onto Ann's hand. It was raining, but they were both secure inside their raincoats and hoods. The rain made the world unusually quiet, and Lena and Ann were unusually quiet as they walked along stepping over puddles. Every so often Lena would release Ann's hand and reach into her cookie box for another animal cracker which she would quickly examine and then stuff whole into her mouth. Her hand free again, she would reach for Ann's hand again. Lena's hand in hers was so small and soft and her grip was so firm that Ann felt unusually happy and secure. She was reminded of when she was a child walking along holding her own mother's hand. "How little your hand is," her mother would remark. Her mother's voice, then, was filled with love and joy. "How little."

The Heavenly Bodies

LENA AND MOLLY were dancing in the center of the floor. Molly was doing a very elementary dance which consisted simply of turning in circles while holding her arms out. Lena was doing a more elaborate dance which consisted of circling Molly. With her arms she made graceful gestures and the expression on her face was one of serious ecstasy. Molly smiled proudly and happily as she turned inside Lena's circle so that the total effect was one of perfect joyful movement and Ann was reminded of how the moon rotates around the earth and how the earth rotates around the sun and now she understood why that was thought to be so lovely.

Passers-by

ANN WAS PUSHING the girls in the double stroller down the street to school. They passed many people as they went and Ann always inspected them to see if they were noticing how unusually beautiful her cargo was, if they had a dog which would be of special interest to Molly or if they looked dangerous—drunks about to collide with them or carpenters with hammers about to fall on them. Most of the people they passed looked quite ordinary and bored, but there was something so mysterious about them nonetheless—perhaps the mere fact of their otherness—that Ann couldn't resist examining them as closely as possible without being conspicuous. Here was a middle-aged woman in uninteresting clothes waiting for a bus. There was no expression on her face. But Ann was not looking at the woman's face. She was looking at her hair—it was pushed back by a plastic headband.

That was how Lena always wore her hair. Lena had a whole box of headbands and every day she selected a different one with which to push back her hair. Could so many days follow one another until Lena was middle aged with a blankness on her face where a brightness now shone? This woman whom they were passing presumably had a life of her own that had a meaning of its own, but Ann couldn't imagine what it could be. Now they were passing an old person, a very old lady with her hair pushed back with a headband, walking somewhere very slowly as if she had some vague destination and her face was utterly opaque as they passed.

A Lesson

ANN WAS PUSHING Lena and Molly to school. It was a warm sticky day even though it was already early October. The weatherman had predicted rain, but there was no rain in sight. A few weeks ago it had been cold and crisp. It had felt wonderful after the hot summer they had had. Leaves had actually started to turn and to fall, and Ann had explained to Lena about autumn and about all the seasons. Now here it was hot again. Ann's clothes were sticking to her uncomfortably. "It's not fall," Lena said.

"Yes it is," Ann said. "See, some leaves are falling even though it is a warm day and most of the leaves are still green." She was very proud of Lena for seeming to comprehend the concept of fall. "It's not fall," Lena said again.

"If it's not fall, what is it? Summer?"

"Yes, it's summer," Lena said.

"No," Ann said. "It's early fall."

"It's summer," Lena said.

Ann had explained to Lena about fall and all the seasons and how they come each year, but she had not explained to Lena that the world is also faltering and inconsistent. "Okay, maybe it's late summer," she said.

Swing Low

ANN AND ABRAHAM were pushing the girls home from the
school picnic. They had had a great time and so they had
stayed too long and now they were overtired. They had ten
blocks to go, and Lena was already starting to scream. Soon
they would both be screaming. Ann started to sing: "Swing
low, sweet chariot." Abraham joined her. He began to har-
monize: "Comin' for to carry me home!" They sang the way
parents have always sung to their children from the beginning of time—to lull them and soothe them and lift their
spirits, to make their little lives like a musical comedy and,
most of all, to drown them out.

Out of Place

ANN WAS OFF on her own going down Broadway. She was not with Lena and Molly chatting with birds and animals in the park. They were home with their daddy. She was going to a class. This was the first meeting. She had not done this before. Suddenly, a squirrel darted across the sidewalk. "Where are you going, squirrel?" Ann asked. What could a squirrel possibly be doing on Broadway?

Weather

IT WAS A PERFECT DAY—blue sky, white puffy clouds. Ann
was pushing the girls to school. She wondered why she felt
like crying. Yesterday the world had been ugly—tired, old,
and broken. Then, as night fell, a storm had risen up from
out of nowhere. A torrent of rain had come and poured over
the town. This morning when the sun rose the beauty of the
world was once again laid bare. Ann wondered how it seemed
to the girls. They rode along in their double stroller eating
grapes and absorbing every nuance and inflection of the at-
mosphere. Did they think that this day was real and yesterday wasn't? And would they be able to hold it in their heads
after it had faded?

Safe at Last

ANN WAS PUTTING the children into their pajamas. They
were the kind of pajamas that had feet, and Ann was reminded of the first time she had seen mothers putting their
children into such pajamas. It was a long time ago, long before
she had had children, long before she had even met Abraham.
It was the time in her life when it didn't seem likely that
she would ever have any children, and sometimes, when she
visited these friends who were mothers, that was a source
of great relief to her. The children were constantly making
messes and running around yelling and screaming. They fell
and they cried. Their noses dripped and they had spaghetti
in their hair. Ann tried to talk with her friends, the mothers,
but they seemed extremely tired and distracted. Night was
falling. It was time for one of the mothers to take her child
home and put him to bed. But since he was likely to fall

asleep in the car, she had brought his pajamas. Now both mothers captured their children and started to undress them. The children lay back on the couch and looked up at their mothers. Their faces were merry as they tried to protest and then succumbed as their mothers tenderly and firmly zipped them into their sleepers. Now as Ann finished zipping Lena and Lena put her arms around her neck Ann remembered how sad and alone she had felt then when those children were finally all safe and secure and cozy at last.

The Life of Luxury

ANN WAS WALKING ALONG with her friend Martha. They
were pushing their children in their strollers to the park.
Martha was a school teacher but was on leave until her
daughter was older. She was telling Ann that her brother-in-
law had just invited them out to dinner to a fancy restaurant,
but she didn't have any shoes to wear. She was thinking of
buying a new pair of shoes. She sounded nervous.

Ann recognized the situation. Here was a woman used to
bringing in money every month. And then she stopped, in
order to take care of her daughter. Therefore, she felt, she
must not spend money on herself. She must dress in rags and
old clothes. She must clean her own house and darn all her
own socks. Ann knew exactly how Martha felt. She needed
new shoes, also, but she was afraid to buy any—despite her
husband's urging. She was afraid she would feel too guilty—

139

because she was not bringing in a paycheck, either, and because, although it was the hardest work she had ever done, looking after her daughters was so rewarding to her that she already felt too self-indulgent, as if she were living a life of utter luxury.

What Did She Know?

ANN WAS DEPRESSED. She had a lot of things on her mind, a lot of things to worry about. She was changing Molly's diaper. Molly looked up at her and giggled. She wriggled away. Ann caught her and she laughed. Her eyes twinkled. Her cheeks dimpled. What did *she* know?

The Sins of the Fathers

ANN WAS DEPRESSED because Abraham was depressed. She couldn't stand it when he was depressed. She felt the whole basis of her existence threatened. If she got depressed enough about it perhaps that would scare it out of him. But she was home alone with the girls. She was having trouble managing them. There was a big bag of garbage in the middle of the floor. There was a funny smell every time she opened the refrigerator. Lena opened the refrigerator and Molly took out the mustard. Ann took it from her and she started to cry. Lena asked for cornflakes. Then she poured them on the floor. "What are you doing?" Ann yelled like a fishwife. Lena started to cry. Molly started to cry. Ann started to cry. Lena looked at her, frightened. "I want my daddy," she said. "I'm sorry," Ann said. "Sometimes mommies get sad, too." Lena came over to her and gave her a hug. Molly came over to her and gave

her a hug. "Thank you, girls," Ann said. "I feel much better."
"You shouldn't cry," Lena said, "because it makes me sad."
"I won't, Lena," Ann said. She felt terrible. Molly and Lena
had had the basis of their existence threatened.

The Oedipal Wars

EVERY NIGHT both Lena and Molly woke up several times. Because she was still nursing, Ann always went to Molly. Abraham always got up with Lena, took her to pee, got her a fresh bottle and lay down in her bed with her. Many mornings Abraham woke up in Lena's bed. He always got up before anybody else. If Lena happened to wake up as he was leaving, he would put her into bed with Ann, and the two of them would cuddle until Molly called them. But this morning Abraham did not leave early. He crawled back into bed with Ann and told her he wasn't feeling well. The children were up, he told her. He was asking her to get up with them. She was worried about Abraham. She wanted to help. But it was hard for her to leap out of bed. Molly had gotten her up three times during the night. She heard a scream. She leaped up and ran down the hall.

After the children had had breakfast they started asking for Daddy. Ann couldn't stop them from running in and jumping into bed with him. Ann went in to wash the breakfast dishes. Then she came back in with two cups of coffee and crawled back into bed with Abraham. She was very sorry that he was feeling sick, but it was a terrific luxury to have him home in the morning.

By this time, the children were playing on the floor. Lena looked up. "No!" she screamed at Ann. "Get out! That's my place!" Ann and Abraham looked at each other. Here was the Oedipus Complex rearing its ugly head. "Get out!" Lena was screaming. She was crying.

"No!" Ann said. "This is Mommy's place." Her inclination was to comply, to humor Lena, but she suspected this might not be healthy for her. "What should we do?" Ann asked Abraham. "I don't think you should give in," he said. "But you could get up and get me another cup of coffee." So Ann got up and Lena got into her place.

Crying for Effect

MOLLY HAD LEARNED how to talk a bit and this gave her a great sense of power. She enunciated very clearly and expressed herself with great style and grace, but nevertheless, people did not always understand her. All they heard was gobbledygook. Then she would start to scream and that was something they could understand.

Sometimes when both children were screaming in hysterical irrational despair Ann remembered screaming that way, too, when she was a child. Then Ann burst into sobs and the children stopped in mid-scream, sobered, suddenly, by the unusual and terrifying sight of their mother in total collapse. It seemed, then, that crying could accomplish something.

A Social Obligation

ANN AND ABRAHAM had invited Magda and her new husband, Blake, to dinner. They had done it because even though neither Ann nor Abraham cared for Magda, Abraham kept running into her and each time he would say, "You and your new husband must come to dinner soon," until it was too embarrassing and Abraham felt he had no choice but to set a date.

Ann worked very hard cooking up a delicious repast. First she burned the vegetables; then she burned the rice. She had asked the butcher to cut up the chicken, but when she unwrapped it to put it in the pan she found it was not divided into the usual drumsticks, thighs, backs, breasts and wings. It had been hacked into less recognizable shapes. Sharp bits of bone protruded. Finally, the tomatoes as she cut them to put them into the salad tasted weird, so she only added a

147

few for color and threw the rest into the garbage. Now the dinner was ready and it was time to dress the children.

She left Molly in her little blue super star suit complete with applesauce but decided to see if she could dress Lena in the exquisite little outfit that had just been handed down to her from her cousins. It had a black velvet skirt, a white imitation silk blouse, and a shiny red vest. Ann followed Lena with it while Lena bounced naked from room to room to room. Lena always preferred to be naked when she was in the house. Perhaps it was because her body temperature was unusually high or perhaps she was simply a wild savage creature.

But for some reason Ann was able to prevail and before the guests arrived she was dressed like a perfect little lady with white tights and a ponytail.

There were a few moments before the guests were due to arrive and the beautiful embroidered vest was shed while Ann set the table. When the doorbell rang both girls were sitting with Ann on the couch drinking apple juice bottles. Molly was pulling open Ann's shirt because she wanted to nurse. Ann did not want her to nurse—Molly was already eighteen months old—but she had not yet figured out a strategy for weaning her. "Nurse," Molly demanded, ripping Ann's shirt open. The guests walked in. As Ann greeted them she felt something wet. Molly was dripping juice from her bottle all down the front of Ann's blouse. There was a large wet circle.

Lena, on the other hand, was a perfect lady and began to make polite conversation with Magda who ooed and aahed over her. Perhaps Magda wasn't that bad, after all, Ann thought. So dinner progressed in a civilized manner except for the fact that Molly kept pointing to things on the table and saying "That! That!" "This?" Ann said, reaching for the Brussels sprouts. "No! That!" Molly screamed. "This?" Ann asked, going for the rice. "No!" Molly screamed. "That!" "No," Ann said. "You've had enough wine." "Nobody's talking to me!" Lena was screaming. Abraham was deep in conversation with Magda over their basic philosophical differences. Ann wondered if Magda was going to cry. She wondered if it was time for dessert. Molly was now throwing her food on the floor. Ann began crawling under the table picking it up, saying "arf! arf!"

Abraham was helping the girls down from their chairs. They had sat at the table long enough. They needed to run about a bit and let off steam. Ann went into the kitchen to make tea. Magda followed her. "Can I help you?" she asked. Ann looked in the teapot. Two roaches were mating in there.

Back in the dining room, Ann passed the cake around. She offered some to Blake. She wondered who he was. He seemed perfectly nice, if rather reserved. "I want some!" Lena called. Ann watched Blake turn around to see Lena stark naked standing on the top of the couch. Even her ponytail had been ripped out. "Cake?" Ann asked.

Now, as the evening wound down, Abraham and Magda continued their discussion with Ann trying to defend Abraham's position and Blake trying to defend Magda's, only his participation was shortly curtailed as Lena placed a large toy called a busy box in his lap and proceeded to manipulate the parts. "Now you do it," Lena said, looking up at him stark naked. "I don't want to," Blake said, weakly. Ann sat comfortably in her chair. No one was bothering her. Molly was reading a little book on the floor at her feet. "You do it!" Lena said to Blake. "He doesn't want to," Ann said to Lena in a voice that Lena would never hear.

"What do you think of Magda now?" Ann asked Abraham when their guests had finally left, pleading fatigue. Abraham was clearing the table, and Ann was collecting the buttons to Lena's mock-silk blouse from the floor. They had popped off when Lena had ripped her shirt off.

"I think she's a pill," Abraham said, spooning the last of the vegetables into his mouth with the serving spoon.

Aloof

IT WAS A PERFECT fall day in the park. Yesterday's rain had washed the window of sky and dropped more brown and bright red leaves to the ground where children could jump in them. When they arrived at the playground they found, however, that only one child had preceded them, a little girl slightly younger than Molly. "Hello, Alma," Ann said to her as she helped Molly and Lena down from the carriage. She was a quiet little girl with a pacifier in her mouth. Lena grabbed a shovel from the bag and began to run around scooping up leaves. Molly ran after her, calling, "Ne-na! Ne-na!" Just then a whole group of children arrived. They were all about Lena's size, and Lena was soon playing with them. Molly called "Ne-na! Ne-na!" but Lena didn't seem to hear her. Molly tried to catch up with Lena, but Lena and the other big children were running too swiftly, spiraling around the playground like so many brightly colored leaves flying in the autumn wind. Ann felt her heart would break. She went to pick Molly up to comfort her, but Molly pushed her away. She began to climb up the slide, a feat a child of her age ought not to be able to do. When she reached the top she turned and looked down on the world.

Hunger for Justice

ANN WAS PUSHING Lena and Molly down the street towards their naps. They had stayed at the playground a little too long. Neither of them had wanted to leave. At first Molly had refused to sit in the stroller—her diaper was wet—and Ann had carried her screaming and kicking while pushing Lena with the other hand. She had finally acquiesced, however, and was riding comfortably. Lena had found the sandwiches in the bag and was just about to finish the last one when Molly turned around, saw this, and began to scream again. "Are you going to eat all those sandwiches yourself?" Ann asked. She wondered what she was doing, talking to Lena that way. Why should she say this when she didn't expect that Lena was capable of sharing, anyway? "Here, Baby," Lena said, handing Molly the last of the sandwich. Molly stopped crying and took it. Ann was very proud of Lena. Molly held the sandwich in her hand, but she didn't eat it.

Ann Regrets Not Sewing
Lena a Costume

IT WAS HALLOWE'EN but Ann hadn't told Lena. There would
be plenty of years ahead when Ann would have to be sewing
little costumes. Lena was too little to go trick or treating and
Molly was certainly too little. There had been a little trouble with the pumpkin—Lena had been visiting at a house
where the little girl had an enormous pumpkin. As they
passed by the vegetable market later that day Lena had
grabbed a little pumpkin from the stack. They had paid for
it and Lena had carried it in her arms all the way home. Ann
was grateful—she couldn't have carried a large pumpkin home
while pushing the double stroller. But when they had arrived
home with it Lena had told her that it was going to grow.
It was going to grow just as big as her friend's pumpkin. Then
Ann had to tell her that it wouldn't grow, it would never

grow any more, but it was very wonderful just as it was. It was a very special little pumpkin. It was the pumpkin she had picked herself. "I love you," said the pumpkin in Ann's falsetto voice.

Then Hallowe'en night came. Ann didn't expect there would be any trick or treaters. She had some candy stowed away just in case, however. Then the doorbell rang. Lena raced to the door ahead of Ann. She was stark naked, as usual. Ann still was unable to keep her dressed in the house. Ann opened the door. There was a gasp from the children, all in costumes.

What We See in Pictures

IT HAD BEEN a trying evening. Molly had screamed all the way home from school. Nothing Ann or Abraham offered her could calm her—bread stick, tangerine, hand to hold. Lena, however, accepted all these bribes and rode along munching and demanding more while Molly screamed and screamed in the seat ahead of her. Passers-by stared disapprovingly as they passed by or stopped to offer free advice. When they finally arrived home Ann sat down on the bed and took Molly in her arms. Molly started to vomit. Ann and Abraham were glad that it wasn't a personality disorder and only a stomach flu which had been making the rounds of the day-care center. Still, they had a lot of vomit to clean up and a lot of laundry to do before they could go to sleep. Lena asked Abraham to read her a book, but as soon as he started reading Molly came running up, screaming "Book! Book!" and grabbing it away until Lena was screaming, also.

Dinner was equally pleasant. Lena insisted upon pouring apple juice into her plate. Molly simply screamed. They fought with toys the rest of the night, throwing them about as Ann picked them up. Finally, they went to sleep. Ann and Abraham tiptoed, still shaken, back to their own room.

Then Ann went to get the package she had picked up at school that day and which she had placed on top a high bookcase to preserve its contents from Lena and Molly. She had been waiting all night for the children to go to bed so that she could take a close look at these new school photos. Now she climbed into bed with them. Abraham got in next to her, and together they stared adoringly at their daughters who sat together on a little red wagon. Lena was smiling up a them with big brown eyes. Molly wasn't smiling at all, but she was nonetheless beautiful.

The Dream

IT HAD BEEN RAINING. Now the sky was grey, warm, thick.
Nothing existed very far away. The world was still unformed.
They sat in the house inside Lena's room: Ann, Lena and
Molly. Ann had thought she would take them out, but
something had happened to the time. It had elongated like
a chain of paper dolls. Meanwhile, space had contracted until
all it held was this brightly colored rug on which they sat.
Molly was playing with the baby clown, cradling him in her
arms and kissing him. Lena was dressing herself in layers of
nightgowns in preparation for the big birthday party. They
babbled quietly and Ann floated, not sorry not to have ven-
tured into the fixed conscious world today. Today a dream
held them in sway.

III. The Foreign Land

The Misplaced Blessing

ANN WAS ON HER WAY HOME to her apartment in Jerusalem when an old lady hailed her on the path. She was very old and lost. She asked Ann for directions and Ann, though she had only been here a week, was able to help her. Ann led her to where she wanted to go, which was just around the corner. The old woman had only been a few feet from her goal all along, but without realizing it. The sun was beating down and she was carrying heavy packages. She was in a foreign country and did not speak the language. She began to bless Ann profusely. But Ann had done very little to help her. Ann had only been the agency of this woman's deliverance; she had actually had very little to do with it. "Bless you! Bless you!" the woman continued to say to Ann as she followed her around the corner. Ann tried to deflect these blessings with her shoulder blades. They made her very uncomfortable. They didn't belong to her.

Molly Falls in Love

FROM THE TIME SHE WAS eighteen months until she was almost two and a half—for almost half of her life—Molly had gone to day-care for a few hours each day. At first she cried when Ann left her, but very soon she looked forward to going each day. She enjoyed the change in environment, she enjoyed playing with the other children, and she had quickly become very fond of the teachers, especially a young woman named Carol. On the way to school she would frequently say to Ann, "I'm going to see my friend Carol!"

The staff at the day-care center was very competent. Ann was especially pleased by the loving environment which they provided. However, summer came, and the school closed for vacation. Ann did her best to keep the girls stimulated, entertained, and out of mischief, but she missed being able to take them to day-care for a few hours each day. They missed it also. Molly, especially, had difficulty understanding about the vacation, and frequently said she missed her friend Carol.

So it was with some hesitation that Ann and Abraham came to the decision to leave New York to spend a year in Jerusalem. Ann worried that it would be too upsetting to the children to yank them out of their school and take them halfway around the world. However, it was a great opportunity for Ann and Abraham.

They began packing up all their things and putting them into storage. They would give up their apartment in Manhattan and get another when they returned. Ann worried that it was going to be traumatic for the children to see everything dismantled and the apartment laid bare. She also worried because Lena's fourth birthday was coming and she didn't know how she would be able to make a party for her in an empty apartment.

"But that's the best place for a party!" her friend Martha suggested. "Simply fill it with balloons. Invite all her friends. They can sit on the floor. They won't care."

So that was what they did. Ann hoped that Lena would now have a happy memory of moving, that this chaotic period would now be contained by ritual and brought into order.

And to make the day special for Molly, also, Ann called up Carol, her teacher, and invited her to come. Ann was a little worried about bothering a teacher outside of school, but Carol assured her that she would be very happy to come. She was, she protested to Ann, as fond of Molly as Molly was of her.

The big day arrived, and everything went as planned. The apartment was completely bare, but they had left a small mattress on the floor of the girls' old room so that Molly could nap before the party. While she was napping, they filled the apartment with balloons and streamers. The doorbell began to ring. Ann and Abraham had invited a lot of their friends, also.

Then Molly's friend Carol arrived. "Thank you so much for coming," Ann said to her. "The pleasure's all mine," Carol assured her. Ann led Carol in to where Molly was sleeping. It was time to wake her.

So Carol helped to wake Molly up. Then together they went out to join the party. They found a nice place to sit under a window, and there they sat, Molly content in Carol's lap, the whole time.

* * *

As it turned out, Molly and Lena adjusted to the move with surprising ease. They loved their new room in their new apartment in their new country almost immediately, and they also loved their new schools and their new teachers. Molly still occasionally mentioned that she missed her friend Carol, and when they played the tape which they had made at the birthday party and Molly heard Carol's voice she looked happy. But mostly she maintained her relationship with Carol in pretend games in which she said that *she* was Carol.

One day, about a month after they had arrived, a letter came for Ann in an unfamiliar handwriting. Ann was surprised when she opened it to see that it was from Carol, Molly's former teacher. Carol had been talking to other teachers in the school, and they had suggested that Molly's attachment to her, Carol, had simply been a way of focusing all her anxiety about the move and the change. They had suggested that when Molly said she missed her friend Carol that she, Ann, should say something like: "I know you miss your friend Carol. And you miss our old apartment, too. And you miss our old playground, too," etc.

Ann put the letter down. She appreciated the fact that Carol had written. She really was a fine person! But there was something wrong about this assessment of the situation by these other teachers who were all extremely well educated but not Molly's favorites. None of them seemed to consider possible what was now clear to Ann—that a two-year-old could fall in love.

What Leads to Speech

IN JERUSALEM, of course, Hebrew was spoken. Abraham spoke Hebrew a little bit and, indeed, they had come here in part so that he might improve his skill in it. Ann spoke Hebrew not at all, but soon after they arrived she enrolled in a class so that she might learn it. It annoyed her that she couldn't understand what the people were saying who sat next to her on the bus or what the newscaster was saying on the television or how much the grocer was saying she owed him. He had to write out the numbers for her, and even then she was often unsure, because the people here had a slightly different style of writing numbers. What made matters worse was that she didn't understand the currency which, because of the inflation, was changing in value every day. But worst of all was how she felt when little children spoke to her, asking her simple questions and looking up into her eyes.

Nonetheless, Ann was glad that there were many children in the building where they were living. Some of them were even Lena's and Molly's ages, though none of them spoke their language. Ann was amazed to see how well Lena was able to play with them. Ann watched her running hand in hand in hand with the sisters who lived beneath them. She would watch from a window while Lena played with sticks in the mud or rode tricycles around and around. And all along she would hear their incessant chatter—the two sisters chirping in Hebrew and Lena also chirping out similar guttural sounds as if she believed that that was all the other girls were doing!

"If only it was true," Ann thought. She hoped that the sisters didn't think Lena too strange, babbling away in this imitation Hebrew like this. Lena had fallen in love with these sisters, no matter that she didn't understand a word that they said. Everyone assured Ann that Lena would be speaking Hebrew within a few months and that she, Ann, although she studied diligently, would not. Indeed, it was true that she was learning very slowly. She felt extremely shy about speaking. Every time she tried to use one of the phrases she had learned it came out wrong or, if she happened to get it right, the person she had spoken to would babble back at her incomprehensibly, and this would be even more upsetting. How could it be that Lena would learn, Ann wondered. She didn't even have grammar to help her. All she had going for her was her passion.

The Net of Human Souls

ANN RODE THE BUS. She found she was staring at a hand. On this hand there were two rings—heavy, gold. One was studded with diamonds—they impressed themselves upon Ann and joined their power with the gold bracelet with which the wrist was laden. The hand was not young. It ended in shining red points. They never worked, they lived only for passion. Or someone, who was not present, loved to see them so.

Ann shifted her gaze. She was now looking at the hip of a girl or a young woman. It was stuffed into pants, but bulging out of them, like longing. Someone, who was not here now, would love this young woman. In the meantime, this extra padding held the place.

Another woman hailed a friend then and caught Ann's attention. She was wearing a white blouse and a plaid skirt. She was smiling. Ann looked down. Her shoes were ladylike and sensible, but out of them rose two thick ankles. When Ann looked up again the woman was still smiling. Perhaps someone, who was not here, loved her neither despite nor because of these ankles.

Ann now saw two men coming towards her. They looked very similar—like brothers. But they didn't appear to know each other. One passed the other by without the slightest glance of recognition. The first began to talk with an old man who might have been his father. The old man spoke warmly to the younger. He was not his father. The younger man spoke respectfully to the old man. His real father did not seem to be here.

Ann found she was thinking of Abraham. He was not here, but she would meet him back at home soon. Thinking of him, she felt buoyant and happy. Suddenly she was possessed with the strong feeling that his love was actually lifting her up, though she was caught in this net of human souls.

His Presence

LENA HAD NEVER WANTED to go to synagogue when they had lived in New York. Sometimes Ann would take her, but she would immediately become squirmy and disruptive, and Ann would spend the entire time outside with her, climbing the stairs to the foyer and then descending the stairs back down again. So Ann left her and Molly at home with a babysitter.

However, now that they were in Jerusalem things were different. Here many children came to synagogue. There was a yard in front where they could play safely if they got too squirmy inside. It was here that Lena met little Baruch, and it was here that they first plighted their troth, though she was only four and he was only six.

In New York Lena had been in love with another little boy, Christopher, but he was already engaged to a four-and-a-half year old named Katrina. This disappointment was now more than made up for by Baruch taking her hand now and declaring his intentions. The older children, the eight year olds and eleven year olds, would come skipping over, laughing, to Ann when she came outside to check on the children to tell her that Lena and Baruch were going to be married. Ann smiled to see them holding hands across the yard.

This was during the High Holidays. Lena and Baruch were able to spend long hours together over the course of many days. Every day on the way home from synagogue Lena would cry that she wanted to go to Baruch's house and Ann and Abraham would explain that she hadn't been invited, but she would see him the next time they came to synagogue. And every morning when Lena woke up she would ask her parents if they were going to synagogue that day and if the answer was no she would cry and protest and become quite impossible.

Finally the holidays ended. When Lena woke up and asked if they were going to synagogue, Ann said no, but to avoid Lena's anguish she suggested that they call Baruch's mother and ask if they could come and visit at Lena's house.

The visit was not as successful as Ann expected. Lena, in her own house where her own possessions were subject to invasion, seemed uncomfortable rather than happy that Baruch was there. Baruch suddenly appeared shy and hid in his mother's skirts.

Nonetheless, after Baruch was gone, and it had seemed to Ann that actually Lena had wanted him to leave the whole time he was there—Lena continued to talk about him—how he was going to take her to outer space—"for real!"—how he was Superman—how she loved him more than she loved Ann, her mother.

"That is how it should be, I suppose," Ann said.

On school days, when Ann and the girls walked home together, Lena would pick up sticks along the way and say that she had to pick them up for Baruch, even though it was

171

silently understood between them that she wouldn't actually be seeing him that day. Molly would pick up sticks, also, imitating her sister, saying *she* was picking up sticks for Baruch. Ann let them chatter on in this way. No day passed without Baruch somehow being mentioned in their chatter and in their play, even though the holidays were over now and Baruch rarely appeared, even at synagogue. Ann wondered if she shouldn't try to get Lena and Baruch together again, but it didn't really seem to be necessary. Lena did not seem to need to see him face to face to have him present.

Who Built This House

"WHO BUILT THIS HOUSE?" Molly, who was now two and a half, asked Ann. Ann was a little surprised by the question. She had to think for a moment before she answered. "A builder built this house," she said. "A builder built this house?" Molly asked. "Yes, a builder built this house," Ann affirmed. And Ann thought that was that. But that night while Ann lay next to Molly on her bed waiting for her to fall asleep, Molly asked again in a whisper, "Did a builder build this house?" "Yes," Ann said, "a builder built this house. Now it's time to go to sleep."

Over the course of several months Molly continued to ask Ann the same question. Ann wondered if Molly did not quite believe Ann's answers or if she simply needed the security of its repetition. Ann did not understand Molly's obsession with this question. She didn't know why Molly couldn't just

173

let the question rest after she had heard the answer.

It was about this time that Lena became ill with a flu bug that kept her home from school for about a week. After the initial high fever had passed and after the doctor had come and affirmed that it was just a flu bug, Ann began to enjoy this peaceful time home alone with Lena. It was on the third morning after Ann had given her her medicine that Lena asked her, "Did God make me sick?" Ann had to think for a moment. "That's an interesting question," she finally said. Molly was very possessive of Ann and screamed whenever Ann tried to hold Lena on her lap. But now Ann and Lena had all these mornings alone together and Ann could hold Lena and lavish her love upon her the way Molly would never otherwise permit. Ann also had the flu at this time. Because of this she had much less energy than she usually had. So she was content to do nothing but take care of Lena, to move in a slower and more limited universe. "Does everybody get sick?" Lena asked. "Yes, everybody gets sick," Ann said. Because, she thought, everybody dies. Ann thought that sickness might be a kind of preparation for death, a constricting of the world. Ann was very good, she realized, at rationalizing sickness and death. Her belief in God's justice and mercy was perhaps too pat. How would she feel if Lena, instead of a flu bug, had some life-threatening illness? Would she be able to maintain her belief in God's justice and mercy then? Could she maintain her faith when she couldn't supply rational arguments for it? Now Ann felt ashamed of her little rationalizations. Who was she to think she could understand God? God was ineffable.

That night when she was putting Molly to sleep Molly turned to her in the dark and asked, "Who built this house?" This time what struck Ann about the question was that Molly presupposed that *somebody* built the house—that it didn't merely exist. "A builder built this house," Ann said. "Oh—a builder built this house?" Molly asked. Ann could hear the wonder in her voice.

To Be in the Present

ANN WAS WAITING for the bus. A storm was brewing. The dark green cypress across the road was beginning to lift up and down. An acquaintance, from her Hebrew class, approached her. "Hello!" he said. But he said it in Hebrew. Actually what he said was "Peace!" "How are you?" he asked her, also using the correct Hebrew idiom. Literally, what he was asking her was "What is (the state of) your peace?" It was interesting to Ann that "at home" in New York when someone asked her how she was she always assumed that they were inquiring about her physical health. It certainly would be considered rude to inquire after the state of another's inner peace. "Fine," Ann answered him, which was what one always said whether one was ill or not. But she said it in Hebrew. Actually, what she said was, "My peace is good." It was appropriate enough, she thought, that in Hebrew one should

175

be so concerned with peace, for the peace here in Israel was constantly threatened by hostile neighbors. But wasn't the state of one's peace always important wherever one was? People did not, in Ann's experience, seem to think so. People seemed to value excitement more. Perhaps people felt more alive when they were in a state of anticipation, Ann thought. People didn't seem to value peace except when they were dying.

The bus came, and, like they say in Hebrew, Ann went up into it. It began to weave through the ancient streets. Inside, the people sat and stood very still. Ann was going over in her head her little Hebrew exchange to see if she had spoken correctly. Actually, she thought, what she had answered was "My peace good," because in Hebrew there was no present tense of the verb "to be." Ann wondered why this was. Was it somehow impossible to realize one's existence in the present moment? Outside the window the sky was darkening. The morning, however, had been bright. The people on the bus sat very still, holding their parcels and looking at nothing. The bus carried them through the stone streets.

An Individual Life

IT WAS CONFUSING to Ann to be in a different country. She didn't know where her home was. Was it possible that she didn't have a home? Did anyone really have a home or was it simply imaginary? It was comforting now to remember how it was when she and Abraham had had a house. From this distance she could see that the house had actually had them. Its driveway was always washing away and it was always wanting culverts dug. Its roof, roofed economically several years previous, was now needing replacing, and first needed removing shingle by shingle. Its French doors were always swelling and refusing to open. God knows what refuse had been left in the dark underneath to slowly rot and eventually shake its very foundations. This "home" of theirs had been hardly more permanent than a human body.

Now they were free of it. They had sold it. They were

eating it. They were living, temporarily, in somebody else's apartment in somebody else's birthplace.

Not that they were just any place—they were in Jerusalem, the eternal city, the city of gold, the heart of the world.

Some days it really felt like that here. But other days, when the skies were holding back rain, Ann saw only emptiness behind the sad masks of the other passengers she was pressed up against on the bus.

Ann was confused about her own existence in time. She had passed her thirty-ninth birthday. What did that mean? Half her life was gone and half, God willing, to come. From the window of this modern apartment on the eastern edge of the city she saw shepherds with goats, donkeys and sheep ringing bells over Mt. Moriah and it was a horizontal time tunnel thousands of years long through which she was being pulled. Simultaneously was she being pulled vertically down through the stones of the Old City walls, impossibly heavy and perfectly cut through the centuries, compressing and connecting year after year of existence so that sometimes it appeared doubtful that she was a particular woman of a particular age in a particular life.

Or perhaps it was precisely in this intersection of horizontal and vertical that she was at last able actually to realize the fact of her existence—her arms opening outwards in an embrace and her legs plummeting downwards to meet the dust.

The Cloud of Time

ANN WAS WATCHING the children. She had just brought them home from school. It was a quarter after one. Abraham would not be home until seven. She had almost six hours to go.

She had no particular activity planned. First there would be lunch, of course. This took only a half hour, even with the usual interruptions of people pooping and Ann going in to wipe them. There were still more than five hours to go. Lena went into the dining room and began drawing with magic markers. Molly followed her. Lena offered to draw a picture of Molly's teacher. Molly thanked her. They weren't fighting. They were playing beautifully. Ann went back into the kitchen to wash the dishes. She wondered why she was counting the hours until the end of the day. She thought about cooking something nice for dinner, but why should

179

she bother? Abraham wouldn't be eating at home. She and the children could just snack. She wandered from room to room, picking up the children's toys as they took them down and interrupting their fights as they broke out. Every so often she looked at her watch and wondered again why she was waiting for the time to go. What was she waiting for anyway? Certainly it would be wonderful when Abraham came home. They would have a few happy hours together and then go to sleep. But what about now? Wasn't she with her children who she loved just as much? And how was the time for them? Were they also waiting for it to pass?

No. They were busy—drawing. Playing mommy and baby, doctor and nurse. Fighting. Dancing together. Now the two little girls who lived downstairs burst in. They were playing flutes, tambourines, xylophones. The music got louder and louder.

Suddenly it was quiet. They had all gone back downstairs to the other girls' house. Was this what Ann had been praying for? She went to the window. It was a beautiful winter day. Ice-white and silver clouds thrust their way above her, spreading and hastening in layers like time. Then, as she watched, the clouds pulled apart and a large open space appeared. Framed inside this space was a dense pure blue presence. But even as Ann watched it began to be obliterated.

Mourning

ANN, HER NEIGHBOR, and their children had just crossed the street from their modern apartment and ascended the low wall to the "mountain" where shepherds still tended their sheep. From here they could see the Dead Sea shining at the foot of the Hills of Moab. Then, when they turned and climbed higher, they could see the ancient walled Old City of Jerusalem with the golden dome of the Moslem Shrine of the Rock and the silver dome of the El Aksa mosque shining above the walls in odd continuation of the gold and silver of the great Second Temple of the Hebrews which lay in ruins beneath them. Ann and her friend watched while their children climbed on the rocks, striving to be "higher than a grown-up."

"My parents are coming for a visit next month," Ann told her friend.

"Are they in good health?" her friend asked.

"Yes, thank God," Ann said. "But my father is seventy and my mother is sixty-six. They won't live forever."

"Does it scare you to think of that?" her friend asked.

"Yes," Ann said. "For one thing, even though my children don't see them very often, they are tremendously significant to them. When Abraham's father died, Lena, who was then two and a half, talked about it every day for a year."

"That must have been tremendously upsetting," Ann's friend said.

"It was," Ann said. "Sometimes I thought about consulting a child psychiatrist. But now I think she was simply the only one in the family who wasn't too inhibited to express what was actually obsessing her. Also, I couldn't help but think that sometimes her daily reminders of him and his death were at *his* request! He was that kind of a person. He commanded that kind of attention."

Ann's friend laughed.

"Of course, Abraham said *Kaddish* for him every day for a year, so maybe what Lena was doing wasn't so very different," Ann said. "But it's funny, I think it was when he stopped saying *Kaddish* that he suffered the worst from losing his father. He said he felt like he had lost his connection to him."

"Were they very close?" Ann's friend asked.

"Well, Abraham lived thousands of miles away from him from the time he graduated college until the year he died. But now he says he feels like an emotional amputee."

"A what?"

"He says he feels like he's cut off from a part of his psyche." Ann looked at her children playing on the rocks and the gold and silver domes shining over the Temple Mount in the distance.

The Part Which No One Sees

THEY HAD COME TO SEE the stalactite caves because a friend
who was an archeologist had said they were smaller than
Carlsbad Cavern but more spectacular. Ann had never been
to Carlsbad Cavern. When they arrived at the parking lot it
was very hot, but they decided to take their coats because
it was bound to be cold in the cave. It was a very long path
down from the parking lot. Molly insisted, as she usually did,
that Ann carry her. Ann was sweating when they got to the
mouth of the cave and looking forward to going in. But first,
the guide told them, they would all go into a special room
to see a movie. This would give them a chance to adjust to
the atmospheric conditions inside the cave. When they
entered the little theater the warm moist air engulfed them.
The movie showed them how stalactites and stalagmites
were formed over countless years drop by drop since way back

before the beginning, but how they were hidden from us until just a few years ago when an earthquake rolled back the rock.

Molly was crying. It was dark. She didn't want to see the movie. So Ann was glad when the movie was over and they were allowed to enter the cave. When they entered the cave they saw a remarkable sight. Only it was the same sight they had seen in the movie, so it wasn't that remarkable. It was very warm and humid inside the cave. So they had to carry their coats. And Ann had to carry Molly. "I want to go home!" Molly was saying. Ann did not like it in the cave either. It was electrically lit so that they could view the stalactites. The guide told them to speak quietly. Molly was screaming. Perhaps a stalactite would come down and pierce them in the head. The guide was pointing to some smaller more stringy formations. "These macaroni-shaped formations are what we call macaroni stalactites," the guide said. "I want some macaroni!" Molly cried. "I'll give you some when we get home," Ann said. "I want to go home and get some macaroni now!" Molly insisted. "In a little bit," Ann said. They were slowly making their way along the path. But the guide kept stopping to show them things. The stalactites, in orange, yellow and red, were everywhere. Ann felt like she was inside a digestive tract. At places the stalactites and stalagmites almost touched, but never would. The guide interpreted this to them as a romantic tragedy. At other places the stalactites shot off at different angles, defying gravity. The guide explaining that they did not have the explanation for this.

Now the guide was pointing out that some of the shapes really looked like a statue of a mother and baby. And here was one that looked exactly like a statue of a Buddha. Ann wondered why the guide needed to impose her idea of what the shapes looked like on them. Why was it necessary to see these shapes, intricate and various as they were, as anything other than bumps? Ann felt a little nauseated. The electric light did not alleviate the feeling of being closed underground,

184

of being somewhere where living beings should not go.

However, as it turned out, Ann and Molly were the only ones who disliked it there. Everyone else had found it beautiful and fascinating.

"But Abraham," Ann said when they were lying in bed in the dark that night, "what is it there for?"

"What do you mean?" he laughed.

"How could it be," she said, "that all these intricate shapes were forming in secret over millions of years? For what? I don't usually question natural wonders. When we went to the Oasis I didn't question it. I could imagine Adam and Eve dipping in the pools and waterfalls there on warm days. But no one ever enjoyed these stalactites before, even though they were always there, right under their feet, since before Adam and Eve."

"The ultra-religious also dislike this cave," Abraham said, "because the geologists date its beginnings from way before the beginning according to the Bible. This cave undermines the basis of their beliefs about creation."

"That's ridiculous," Ann said. "But what do you think?"

"What do I think?" Abraham asked. "I like the cave. It's a good example of what I believe."

"But surely you don't belive that things are simply created because of random natural phenomena without purpose or meaning?" Ann asked.

"Of course not," Abraham said. "The cave reminded me of what I know about Buddhist statues."

"Buddhist statues?"

"When Buddhists make their statues," Abraham said, "they finish them perfectly on the insides as well as the outsides. They paint the insides, the part which no one sees."

Worries About the Future (I)

IT WAS A PERFECT DAY. The sky was a crystalline blue, the
air was crisp, and the occasional sonic boom only served as
a reminder of how peaceful and quiet the world was. Ann
was walking the children to school. As they walked they were
greeted by neighbors and friends. Ann was proud of her
children. She was proud of the way Molly sang a little song
as she walked along and proud of the way Lena skipped. She
said good-by to them at their schools and started to walk
home alone. She was very depressed.

It had nothing to do, she was sure, with her relationship
with Abraham. Of that she felt secure. Only that morning
he had told her again how beautiful she was to him. She
thanked God every day for bringing him to her. At night when
they were alone in the dark she could bare her soul to him
without inhibition. And he would freely reveal himself to

186

her; to her he was all silver and golden and woven in infinite intricacy. And yet, she realized now, there was something in her which had drawn away of late, something which was at a distance from herself and therefore Abraham as well.

What was it that was bringing her so low? Perhaps it was that she was coming down with a cold. But she still walked unimpeded up the stairs while the old lady who had come in the front door with her labored painfully behind. Could it be that she was worrying about money? Certainly it was true that some unexpected expenses had come up recently and it wasn't exactly clear to them how they were going to handle them. But she knew they would somehow. They always did. And money was always there to worry about. What was she worrying about today in this beautiful world full of faces that had become both familiar and dear?

In a little over three months they would probably not be here. It wasn't clear where they would be. That was the problem. There was a good possibility that they would return to their old neighborhood in Manhattan. They were waiting to hear if an apartment had become available. There was also a possibility that Abraham would have a job in another part of the state and they would all move there. If none of these possibilities came through they possibly could remain in Jerusalem one more year, but they would have to find another apartment and it would probably be in another part of the city. Perhaps if she knew what was to come she would feel better, but the only thing that was for certain was that they were leaving this world.

Of course, they had known all along that they wouldn't be here forever. But at first, when the faces and the stones and the sounds of the birds were coming into focus that had not seemed real. Ann found she was thinking about Abraham's father, Isaac, and the month that he had died. It was about this time of year, two years ago, when he had first gone into the hospital. Ann and Abraham had each held onto

187

one of his hands. "Why are you holding on so tight?" he had asked. "I'm not going anywhere."

They brought the children to visit him frequently. The children were the world to him. He doted on them. Lena had climbed up into his bed with him and had shared his lunch. He had watched Molly take her first steps across the floor of his room. These things brought him great joy. But one day he asked that they no longer bring the children. It was too much for him. After that his deterioration was rapid, and within a few weeks he was dead.

Worries About the Future (II)

STEVE AND ARLENE, a pleasant young couple, were visiting Ann. They were expecting their first baby and were very excited. They joked about the funny names they would give it. Their pregnancy made Ann feel happy. There was nothing more wonderful to her. She remembered the joy she had felt when she was first pregnant. She suspected that Steve and Arlene had come not just to visit her, but to see her children, to get an idea of what was in store for them.

Lena had just discovered stapling and was busy drawing pictures, cutting them out, and stapling them together. Ann was very proud of how clever and charming she was. Molly was doing a little Molly dance, running around in a circle. Lena picked up Molly's favorite green pen and began to draw with it. Molly began to scream. "Be sure to get a good pair of earplugs," Ann joked to Steve and Arlene.

"I was never around babies growing up," Arlene said. "I was the youngest. I don't even know how to diaper a baby! I'm really afraid I'm not going to be able to handle the diapers."

"Diapers are nothing," Ann said. "Diapers are the least of it. Don't worry about diapers!"

"What *should* we worry about then? What is the worst of it?" Arlene asked. She looked worried.

Ann had to think. Was it waking up with them in the night for years and years? Was it worrying about them when they were sick or unhappy at school? Or missing them when they were away from her or hating them when they continuously took apart what she was trying to put together? Was it how the old significance of her life had melted away in the face of this relentless responsibility and preoccupation? Was it that the world was changed utterly and would never be the same again or the terror she now felt about the possibility of her own death when her children needed her so?

"Nothing," Ann said, looking steadily at Arlene. "There's nothing to worry about."

Home

ANN HAD LIVED in the same house in the same small town in Northern California for ten years before she and Abraham decided to move to New York. She knew where to go to get shoes repaired there, where to buy fresh fish, and she knew everyone in the town. She knew who had once been married to whom, who had had a mental breakdown five years back, and who, though he had shown so much early promise, had so thoroughly botched his life that any newcomer to the community would only perceive him as an ordinary failure. Ann knew, also, what to expect from the weather and hence from the flora of this little paradise. This expectation was based on the tremendous rains which characterized her first winter there and the magnificent ocean of wildflowers which revealed itself to her that first spring when the ocean of rain was carried back up to the heavens. That first summer was characteristically hot, so that when subsequent summers were uncharacteristically cool, and subsequent winters were uncharacteristically dry, and a blight withered the blossoms of subsequent springs Ann felt the world falling from grace. That first spring, when the white blossoms had started to drift down, Ann had vowed to be buried under the apple tree that stood close to the top of the hill. But one year that apple tree fell over in a freak storm. As it turned out, it had been hollow. Now Ann wanted to take back her vow.

When she and Abraham decided to move to New York many people in the community had come to help them pack and to take care of their affairs. Then Ann saw that these were good people, that they had many good friends here. But they hadn't been settled more than a few weeks in their new apartment in New York when Ann could see that all these dear old friends might be stuck in the trap of their lives, unable to imagine that the world existed outside. And Ann pitied them.

Meanwhile, she was discovering where to go to get fresh fish and how to get her shoes repaired. Soon enough, she was becoming familiar with everyone in the community. She was even able to develop a few close friendships. She had more in common with these new friends than she now had with the people back in California. When she thought of her old friends now she felt sad. She mourned. It was as if she herself had died. But mostly, she was becoming more and more involved with the new community, seeing, and seeing through these new people.

Perhaps she herself was the one who was transparent. She often felt wispy and insubstantial, because she had no clear idea about what her grounds were. So since she already felt homeless she didn't think it would be too big a wrench for them all to pack up, after only two years in New York, and go for a year to another country.

That first winter in New York had been mild, contrary to

their expectations, but the first summer had been brutally hot. It was the following spring that they reached their decision to leave.

Ann had been dreading summer's coming all year, but knowing that they would be leaving as soon as it was over somehow made it more bearable.

It was a beautiful summer. The air was clear and it was never too hot. All their friends from the community came to help them get ready to move. Ann realized that these were good people. She was fond of them.

But once she was settled in her new apartment in Jerusalem it was easy to see that all her friends back in New York were, perhaps, artificially stuck in their lives. She didn't understand why they didn't all come here where it was, obviously, better to live.

Very soon Ann found where to buy fish. She had her shoes repaired, despite the language barrier. Some things are universal. What made the move most smooth, perhaps, was that they moved into a lovely community of other expatriates.

Most of these people had lived in this neighborhood and had been interacting with each other for about ten years. Within a few months Ann was able to see who here was really following his heart's desire and who had had to compromise along the way. She learned the history of their relationships, and was soon enough privy to their petty disputes and jealousies. She felt herself in a privileged position, because she did not really live here. It was easy enough for her to see through these people. She saw them, again, as artificially limited by their situations. They didn't see, as she did, that the world existed outside and in spite of them.

And then the first rains came. Ann didn't know what to expect. It was cozy inside their apartment. But this wasn't their apartment. It and all the things in it belonged to another family who had gone to still another country for a year. Ann found she was crying, because she didn't have a home.

193

On Determinism and Free Will

WHEN AN APARTMENT in Manhattan was offered to Ann and Abraham they realized that they had no choice but to accept it. It was a rare and wonderful event to find an apartment of a reasonable size for a reasonable rent right where they needed to live. Ann and Abraham took this as a message from God that they should now return to their pursuits in New York rather than try to live in Jerusalem another year. Last year, when they had lost their old apartment in Manhattan, they had taken it as a message to come to Jerusalem.

Ann and Abraham were both prone to seeing signs from God everywhere. For example, every year when they got their new calendar they looked at the pictures for each month to see how that month would be. It was wonderful to them to see how the pictures always predicted their lives. For example, the month they had moved from California there had been a picture of a hot air balloon taking off. They had laughed and said how appropriate it was. Then the day of their actual departure came. They sat outside saying good-by to the house. And while they were sitting, an actual hot-air balloon exactly like the one on their calendar came and hovered over them.

When they came to April on this year's calendar there was a photographic study of a girl climbing up on a chair and jumping off. "Look," Ann had said, "this is me getting ready for Passover!" There was a lot of work to do to get ready for Passover and Ann did have to climb up on chairs to clean and to get things down—exactly like in the calendar. Of course, she also had to do a lot of other things which she didn't see in the calendar—like roll up the rugs.

Passover came and went. Finally, everything was back to normal. One afternoon Lena suggested to Molly that they do their jumping trick which they hadn't done for some time. She pulled two chairs to the middle of the floor. "Be careful!" Ann said. She knew they were going to find the tile floor very hard now without the padding of the rug which had been rolled up since Passover. "Be careful!" she said as they leapt and fell.

Molly was screaming. Ann held her in her arms. She screamed and screamed. She wouldn't stop. They took her to the emergency hospital. The x-ray showed nothing. But she wouldn't walk.

When she couldn't walk a few days later they took her to their pediatrician. He found nothing and sent them to a specialist. The specialist found nothing, but sent them to get a blood test. Ann was wandering around the corridors of the hospital looking for the laboratory while Molly screamed in her arms. Molly didn't want to get a blood test. Tears ran freely down Ann's face.

That night when Molly was asleep Ann went into the kitchen to make Lena's lunch for the next day. She found

195

she was looking at the calendar again. A chill ran through her. There was the girl—Molly!—climbing up on a chair and jumping off. Why hadn't she seen this before? It wasn't her, Ann, getting ready for Passover at all, it was a picture of Molly's accident! No, that wasn't true. It was both.

For a minute, Ann found herself hating the calendar. Because she felt, irrationally, that she should have seen this before and she should have prevented Molly from jumping. She had known that she had rolled up the rug and that the floor was hard and that the children would not realize this. It had been in her power to prevent this accident, but all she had said was "be careful." Because she was tired and harried at that moment and because it would have taken an extra burst of energy, some force of will, to overcome the inertia of that moment which had already been determined and published in the calendar.

Calling the Children to Sleep

ANN WATCHED out the window unnoticed. It had become darker inside the house than it was out. The children were playing down below in the yard with the other children from the building. They were running and jumping gleefully. Molly moved perfectly, as if she had never hurt her leg. It was strange to think that in just a few weeks they would be back in New York and the children would no longer be able to play with these others with whom they had grown so close. Theoretically these others would still be here on the grass, but there would be an empty space where Lena and Molly had been. And for Lena and Molly, Ann feared, it would be, perhaps, as if they had died.

They had been playing on this grass together every day. While they were playing, the bushes which at first had looked so ordinary, had burst into gorgeous bloom. A heady perfume

197

had filled the air. While Ann watched from the window, birds flew back and forth from the trees to the window ledges opposite. Then a great breeze had risen up and inhabited the trees and moved them like loving arms over the voices of the children. But the darkness was falling. Ann strained to see, but she could not. Then she heard voices calling the children in to sleep.

Leaving This World

ANN WAS VERY SAD about leaving Jerusalem. She had many good reasons for wanting to stay, but the real reasons were irrational—a certain smell that came out of the stones the city was built of, the texture of the air, a strange feeling of comfort. Every minute here was precious now. Ann walked around with a lump in her throat. She appreciated every moment now and saw nothing bad, like a person sentenced to die.

Abraham, also, was sad to leave. Like Ann, he also wished that they would return here to live one day, but he knew the chance of that happening in the near future was very remote. Since he knew that they were leaving in a very short time he had difficulty feeling here at all. Emotionally, he was already gone. In his imagination he was arranging the books on the shelf of a bookcase in the world to come.

199

IV. The Face Appears

Justification

IT HAD ALREADY TAKEN enormous energy to put on their tights, leg-warmers, snowpants, sweaters, hats, mittens, coats, scarves and boots. They had to return to the house to retrieve a doll in order to leave it on the bus. "Who's child is this?" the fat lady standing on the bus said. She meant Molly. "She should be taught her manners. She should stand on the bus and give her seat to her elders." "She's only three," Ann said, standing. "She's old enough," the fat lady yelled. The little old ladies smiled and winked. Molly started to scream, "I'm not three! I'm not three! I'm three and two thirds!" Molly's age was very important to her. She spent a lot of time thinking about it.

That actually was an event from another day. This day didn't have any events to justify it. But at least it was over. Then the doorbell rang.

Their neighbor was very excited. She had just come from an art gallery. There had been an exhibit of photographs from Israel. There was a Yemenite bride and an Ethiopian man and Lena and Molly. "These are my neighbors," their neighbor had told the curator. "These are Israeli children," the curator had corrected.

The bedtime story Ann told that night was about two little girls named Sally and Sena. This winter Sally and Sena were living in New York. But last spring Sally and Sena were in Israel. One day when they were still in Israel there was a vacation from school. Their mommy decided to take them downtown on the bus. She had read that there was going to be an art exhibit. They got off at the wrong stop. It was hot. They had to walk. The girls were thirsty. The exhibit was not interesting. They sat in the courtyard drinking sodas. A woman asked Ann if she could take the girls' picture. Ann said yes. This had happened before. Ann had said yes. They left and wandered about aimlessly. They arrived home without any events to justify the day.

"I hate this story," Lena said.

"But later," Ann continued mercilessly, "when the girls were living in New York, their neighbor came to tell them that every day has something significant, something meaningful about it, even if we're not aware of it at the time."

"I hate this story," Molly said.

"And then everybody went to sleep in their cozy little beds," Ann said.

The next Sunday, Ann, Abraham, Lena and Molly all took the subway to the art gallery. They found the picture of Lena and Molly. It was a beautiful print. But it was not very good of Molly and Lena. Ann wished she had brushed their hair. The print was selling for sixty dollars. They didn't buy it. Ann wondered who would. It was strange to her to think that someone would want to have a picture of her children hanging in their living room. But of course, this picture wasn't really of their children. Their children were just the photographer's material. It was how the photographer composed and developed the image that made it into something that transcended these mere children. Therefore, Ann and Abraham didn't feel they had to buy it.

They bought a few tapes and toys in the shop, however, and with these new things they were able to fill out the rest of the Sunday, and then it was over.

What They Don't See Won't Help Them

LENA HAD FALLEN IN LOVE. She had discovered a little girl who lived in their building and this girl had discovered her. Laurie was six—a year older than Lena, but this didn't matter—they were a perfect match. They both loved to draw and loved to dance and loved to dress up. It had been love at first sight. They played happily for hours, and when apart they drew pictures for each other and wrote each other letters. "Dear Lena," Laurie wrote, "I love that I have a frend. I was lonlee. I love you." Lena drew a picture of a girl with starry eyes for Laurie. There were flowers with smiles in the picture and Laurie's name and age inscribed there.

Ann and Abraham were delighted with this relationship. They found it especially sweet that they had mythologized their love. Both girls claimed that they had actually met many years ago, when Lena was two and Laurie was three. They

206

had met in school, they said. This was, of course, impossible. They had never gone to the same school. But Ann and Abraham didn't tell them this. They understood how they felt. Didn't they also believe that they had met earlier in life? Hadn't they figured out that both their parents had taken them to visit the same country to stay in the same hotel the same year? Didn't they believe that they must always have known each other since their love was eternal?

Ann was trying to explain all this to her friend Leah who had come to visit unexpectedly from Boston. But she didn't know if Leah could understand because Leah had not found the love of her life yet.

Ann had wondered if Leah wasn't going to get together with Abraham's friend, Jon, because Leah and Jon had seemed to really hit it off the last time Leah had visited. But that had been almost two years ago. As it turned out, Leah had not forgotten him, and she asked after him, but Ann had to tell her that they hadn't seen him for almost a year and weren't even sure if he still lived in the neighborhood.

The doorbell was ringing. It was Jon. He was sorry to drop in on them like this. He just wanted to return a book he had borrowed from Abraham a year ago. He was surprised and delighted to see that Leah was visiting and she was equally happy to see him. Ann pressed him to come in and stay for dinner.

Ann found it quite remarkable that they had arrived out of the blue at the same time, but Leah and Jon seemed to think it was just a lucky coincidence. At dinner the conversation was general, but it was clear to Ann and Abraham that Leah and Jon were really only speaking to each other. They seemed in perfect agreement and even mirrored each other's opinions. Ann wondered if they were a match, if God had brought them together. But Leah and Jon didn't think God worked that way. God had started everything in motion, of course, but God wasn't personally involved in little details of little people's lives.

Ann was disappointed. She had hoped that they would get together. Perhaps they were right about God, she thought. Perhaps He was limited in some way, after all. Maybe all He could do was lead the horse to water.

What They Don't See Won't Hurt Them

THEY WANTED TO do something really special to celebrate Abraham's birthday, but when they looked in the paper they couldn't find any movies or concerts that really appealed to them. They thought they would just get a babysitter and go out to dinner to their favorite Chinese restaurant, but when they thought about it, for the price of the babysitter they could take the children with them, so that is what they decided to do. The children loved to go out to dinner and they were very excited about it and they realized that having everyone together would make the occasion that much more special. To cap it off they would go up the Empire State Building. It was just a block from the restaurant, and if they ate early enough they would hit the Empire State Building right at the perfect time, just as dusk was fading into night.

The girls were really excited and ran all the way to the bus.

Molly, unfortunately, fell asleep when they had gone just five minutes of their half-hour bus trip. Ann hoped that Molly would wake up as she carried her off the bus, but she didn't. It was several blocks from the bus stop to the restaurant, and Ann spoke in Molly's ear as she carried her, but Molly snored on. Ann wanted her to wake up. She was dead weight in her arms.

At the restaurant they were given a booth, and she was able to lay Molly down. She tried to awaken her all through the hors d'oeuvres but it was to no avail. Finally, Ann began dipping her fingers in the ice water and putting them on Molly's temples. Molly began to stir. Then she sat up and looked around, her eyes wide open. They had already finished half their dinner. They had come all the way down Fifth Avenue on the bus and walked several blocks in a strange neighborhood, but Molly could not possibly know how they had gotten here or where they were. However, this did not seem to bother her and she began to eat.

After dinner they walked to the Empire State Building. Abraham was hurrying them along because he knew the timing was crucial. Ann and Abraham loved the top of the Empire State Building because they were afraid heights. But the top of the Empire State Building was all fenced and glassed in. So they could enjoy the thrill of the view without the feeling of danger. Still, when Ann set the children up on ledges so that they could see, albeit the ledges were behind bars, Ann couldn't help but remember stories she had heard as a child of suicides jumping off the Empire State Building.

She remembered something that had happened several years ago when they had lived in another building. In that building, the girls' room had been in the back facing on the court. As she sat in that room playing with the girls on hot summer evenings with the window open she could hear voices calling from the other apartments which also backed onto this court. She did not like hearing these voices, but there was no way to avoid them. Several days in a row she had to listen to the moans of a man in some sort of ecstasy. There was only his voice, never a sound from any partner. Ann hoped that the girls weren't noticing these strange rhythmic moans. It seemed wrong to involve little children in this. But that wasn't the worst of what they heard.

One evening the three of them were playing on the floor with blocks when they heard a voice calling desperately, calling to someone who wouldn't answer. Then there was a terrible scream, the scream of someone falling out a window and then the terrible thud, the thump, and the terrible silence.

The voice then started to call again—hoarsely, loudly, but of course there was no answer.

The next day Ann heard that indeed a woman had fallen out a window. She had died. Ann didn't tell the girls. She hoped they hadn't been aware of what had happened. She always told them not to get near the windows. There were guard rails up, but she didn't trust the guard rails.

She didn't trust the guard rails here at the Empire State Building and held on to the children as they peered over the side. "Look!" Lena said, pointing into the sky. "Fireworks!" "Where?" Molly asked. She wanted to see the fireworks. "Isn't that beautiful!" Abraham said. "It must be for my birthday."

There was something about these fireworks that was not beautiful to Ann. There was something about them that chilled her. Something that wasn't quite right. "I can't figure out where that is," Abraham said. "Is that Shea Stadium over there?"

Had they not listened to the news later that night they would not have known that they had witnessed a plane crash, and that what they had seen which to them had looked so beautiful and so distant was the sight of people dying.

Ann did not read any of the news reports which described who the people were who had died in that instant or how it had come to happen, and she certainly didn't mention it to the children, but nonetheless, that burst of light in the sky haunted her like the sound of the scream which fell into the nothingness and she wondered why it was that she was brought to participate in this death.

The Courage to Face the World

MOLLY HAD HAD A difficult time adjusting to school this year. Her old friend Debra was in the class, and Ann had thought that this would have made her feel secure. But although Molly liked Debra, they didn't really play well together. Debra was a lot bigger than Molly and always tried to lead. Molly, who was always so boisterous at home, was now shy and quiet at school. She played alone — although not unhappily, and did not easily join in with the other children. Ann felt it was all right if she wanted to play alone, but felt better when Molly made an attachment to one of the teachers, who happened to have the same name as Ann. Ann-the-teacher was intelligent and sensitive, and Ann was proud of Molly for choosing such a worthy object for her love. Molly followed Ann-the-teacher everywhere, and allowed her to integrate her into activities with the other children.

It was about this time that Ann took Molly for her interview with the psychologist at Lena's school. All children had to be interviewed by the psychologist before they could be admitted to Lena's school, and Ann hoped that Molly would be able to go there next year. Except for Ann-the-teacher, Ann was not at all happy with the school where Molly was, and wanted Molly to be with Lena in a more secure environment.

Molly was very shy with the psychologist and would barely look at her or talk to her. The psychologist asked her to draw a face. "I can't," Molly said in a very small voice.

Nonetheless, Molly passed the test. But Ann wondered if she should be drawing faces already, and not the scribble scrabble which she always did. Ann tried to remember how old Lena had been when she had first started to draw faces. To do a drawing of a face one would have to be able to think symbolically. A drawing of a face was two-dimensional and made out of crayon and paper. Faces are really three-dimensional and made out of flesh and blood. Of course, Ann thought, Molly could think symbolically. She could hold a picture of a zebra in her hand and know it was a picture and not a real zebra. Then what could bring Molly to the realization that she had the power to create something which could stand for something else? Was motor coordination the problem, or had she never thought to do it?

The next day when Ann came to get Molly at school Ann-the-teacher told her that Molly had made a new friend. In fact, they were inseparable. He had brought out a side of her which they had never seen. With him she now ran and played gleefully.

His name was Martin, and he was from South America. When he had first started school a few months ago he could only speak Spanish, but now he had learned enough English to get along. Ann wondered if Molly had felt sympathy for him because last year she had been in a country where no one spoke her language and she had had to learn a new one.

214

The next day when Ann came for Molly, Martin came up to her and gave her a hug and a kiss. Ann met Martin's mother, and since a school holiday was coming, they arranged a playdate.

Their first date was at Martin's house. Ann walked Molly over, but Molly did not want her to come in with her. Ann found this very unusual and independent of her.

The next time, Martin came to Molly's house. They really did play beautifully, and seemed extremely happy together. After a while, Ann gave them some crayons and paper. Martin scribbled large circles with great energy. Then Molly drew a face. She even put in eyebrows. Then she drew a body and arms, legs, feet and hands. Ann couldn't believe what she was seeing. Then Molly, almost bursting with pride and joy, drew another—and another. And then she drew a king and queen.

Ann was astounded that Molly, who had not even been able to draw a face the day before should suddenly be able to draw not only a face with all the features but a complete figure as well. She wondered how this could have happened.

There was one aspect of these drawings, she noticed then, that was not anatomically correct. The heads were not located on the top of the bodies but instead were in the center. Ann pointed this out to Molly. So she added a half-circle on top of the whole circle of the body. But this half-circle did not contain the features. The eyes, the windows of the soul, and the mouths, opening to express their love, remained located in the face which stayed in the center of the body where the heart might be.

Printed December 1987 in Santa Barbara & Ann Arbor
for the Black Sparrow Press by Graham Mackintosh
& Edwards Brothers Inc. Design by Barbara Martin.
This edition is published in paper wrappers; there
are 250 hardcover trade copies; 150 copies have
been numbered & signed by the author; & 26 lettered
copies have been handbound in boards by Earle Gray,
each with an original drawing by Sherril Jaffe.